Picture the MI5 archives, if you will – a gloomy, dusty catacomb devoted to the interment of a hundred years' worth of classified documents. In the corner, a locked door, because although everything down here is secret, the contents of this room are *really* secret. A sign on the door reads THE DISCIPLINE FILES. Inside, there is clearly more material than anyone ever anticipated. Shelves are buckling, cardboard boxes spilling their contents onto the floor. Because they have a discipline problem, our spies, or so recent history would suggest.

In *Beside the Syrian Sea*, an analyst steals hundreds of stolen documents and resurfaces in Beirut, desperate to negotiate for the release of his kidnapped father...

In *How to Betray Your Country*, a disgraced agent-runner in emotional free fall tries to build a new life in Istanbul, only to stumble across a mysterious Islamic State figure who is not quite what he seems...

In *The Man in the Corduroy Suit*, a talented interrogator looks into the suspected poisoning of a retired colleague, but a startling discovery forces him to choose between obeying his masters or his own conscience...

Three stand-alone stories, three spies, one very serious problem. In this day and age, with the meaning of duty, tradition and loyalty increasingly open to interpretation, how do you make sure your spies do what they're told? And what do you do when they don't?

THE MAN
IN THE
CORDUROY
SUIT

James Wolff

BITTER LEMON PRESS
LONDON

BITTER LEMON PRESS

First published in the United Kingdom in 2023 by
Bitter Lemon Press, 47 Wilmington Square, London WC1X OET

www.bitterlemonpress.com

The first extract quoted on page 224 is taken from
'Dulce Et Decorum Est' in Wilfred Owen, *Poems*, Chatto & Windus, 1920.

The second extract quoted on the same page is taken from Friedrich Nietzsche,
Human, All Too Human, Penguin Classics, 1994.

A CIP record for this book is available from the British Library.

ISBN 978–1–913394–84-4
eBook ISBN USC 978–1–913394–85-1
eBook ISBN RoW 978-1-913394-86-8

Typeset by Tetragon, London
Printed and bound in Great Britain by CPI Group (UK) Ltd Croydon, CRO 4YY

For my children, who remind me every day just how nimble and funny language can be, with more love than this tongue-tied father can hope to put into words.

PROLOGUE

CONFIDENTIAL

FROM: Metropolitan Police
TO: MI5 (Lead Development)
SUBJECT: Incident 287466
DATE: 8 May 2019

1. We are writing to inform you that a 64-year-old woman named Willa KARLSSON was admitted to University College Hospital last night in an unconscious state. KARLSSON presents a number of unusual symptoms. For this reason her doctors have been unable to reach any agreement on a diagnosis, but we have been told that one of the possibilities under serious consideration is that she has been the victim of a poisoning.

2. Paramedics were sent to her south London address at 2135 following a call from a downstairs neighbour who reported hearing a loud noise that sounded like a fall. A uniformed police officer who attended the scene observed no signs of violence or forced entry. The neighbour said that KARLSSON lived alone, and described her as quiet, unremarkable and having the dishevelled and careless appearance of a "bag lady".

3. In light of the medical assessment, which doctors characterize as "tentative and rapidly evolving", our officers have discreetly secured the property and moved residents of the building to a nearby location while experts from Porton Down carry out a thorough examination for traces of poison. Early reports suggest that none has been found, and we note that the paramedics and the police officer who attended the scene last night are all in good health (although they remain subject to close monitoring).

4. An out-of-date identity card found in KARLSSON's flat indicates that she was until last year an employee of British intelligence. We would like to arrange a meeting with you as a matter of urgency to discuss the possible relevance of this to our investigation.

5. Regards.

CONFIDENTIAL

CHAPTER ONE

Monday, 0900

1

It might come as a disappointment to learn that the natural habitat of the intelligence officer is not the shooting range or the gym mat, the departure lounge of a hot and dusty airport, the safe house or the interrogation cell. It's not halfway up a ladder aimed at the draughty rear window of a foreign embassy. It's not even the street, the simple street – narrow, damply cobbled, thick with London fog and Russian menace. No, the natural habitat of the intelligence officer is the meeting room. Spies like to talk.

"You will have heard of a section called Gatekeeping," says Charles Remnant. "In simple terms, we investigate the insider threat – the threat posed by our own members of staff, who may have been recruited by hostile foreign powers. What you will not have heard of, however, unless matters have really got out of hand, is the secret cadre of officers we refer to as Gatekeepers."

In this case, not just any meeting room, but one at the top of the building, one at the dead end of a corridor otherwise used to store broken filing cabinets and unused safes. The paint is peeling, the floor stained brown with water from a burst pipe. A sign on the door states ELEC-TRICAL EQUIPMENT: STRICTLY NO ADMITTANCE. Leonard Flood has worked in the building for seven years and wasn't aware of its existence until this morning. Dark blue carpet, white walls, two office chairs equipped with the usual array of levers, knobs, switches and even a small hand pump to control air pressure across the lumbar region. He recalls watching the skittery fingers of a new recruit on another floor discover by chance an unexpected button under an armrest, and her panic at the thought she had accidentally triggered a silent alarm or hidden recording device rather than made an imperceptible adjustment to the angle of her seat.

Leonard makes people nervous, despite his best intentions. Even when, as on this particular Monday morning, he is the younger of the two officers in the room by at least twenty years, the more junior by several grades, the one who has been summoned to the meeting not by email or phone, as might have been expected, but by a quiet word in his ear from a guard as he came through the security pods to begin his working day.

"I cannot overemphasize the sensitivity of what we are about to discuss," says Charles Remnant. He smiles tightly to show he appreciates that in this building everyone says such things all the time, but then frowns to make clear that on *this* occasion the words must be taken very seriously indeed. Thirty years clear of the military and he wears his tweed jacket and regimental tie as though the whole damn get-up is unforgivably casual.

It is the first time Leonard has been this close to him. The distance Remnant carefully places between himself and his colleagues has created a space where truths and untruths can grow wild: that he has his lunch carried up from the canteen on a silver tray, that he has curated a vast compendium of staff misbehaviour he refers to in private as The Discipline Files, that he lost his left eye in an accident involving shrapnel, a champagne cork, a swan, a bayonet. At this distance, Leonard thinks, judging from the pattern of scars, the truth is probably more prosaic: that someone once screwed a pint glass into his face.

"The concept is simple," Remnant is saying. "Gatekeepers are officers who carry out covert investigations into fellow members of the intelligence community – into their colleagues and friends, let's not beat around the bush – to ascertain whether or not they pose a threat to national security. Is that clear?"

"Everyone has heard of Gatekeeping," says Leonard. "Everyone accepts that the office has to investigate leaks, misconduct, penetration by hostile agencies. Why is the existence of the Gatekeeper cadre so sensitive?"

"You're in this room because people tell me you're clever. What do *you* think is the answer?" The unspoken word *soldier* hovers at the end of every question Remnant asks.

Leonard turns his face to the window. It is the beginning of a long, hot English summer. Light hums indistinctly but fiercely through the reinforced glass. "You're talking about a network of informers who maintain a constant watching brief on those around them," he says.

"They spy on the spies, in other words. Which means they must be embedded throughout the office, in every department, carrying out their regular duties in addition to their covert work as Gatekeepers. Your own secret army of accountants, investigators, locksmiths, surveillance —"

"You'll understand I can't possibly confirm —"

"I don't know what you expect your Gatekeepers to see," says Leonard. "Anyone carrying out an act of betrayal wouldn't do it in plain sight. Unless this is an espionage version of the broken windows theory. The person who goes on to sell secrets to the Chinese will at some point along the way steal an envelope from the stationery cupboard."

"Don't be facetious, Leonard. I'm not here to justify the programme – it has already been extremely successful. I'm here to tell you that you are now part of it."

"I'm not being facetious. How many of us are there?"

Remnant is taken aback by the pronoun, by the speed of the pivot, the military swivel, worthy of a parade ground. The truth is that Leonard has already pinned this appointment to his swelling chest. He is proud to learn he is a Gatekeeper, even if he will never be allowed to wear the honour in public, even if he is not yet entirely sure what it will require of him, or how it will change his life forever in a matter of days. "How many?" Remnant asks. "Well, I don't know exactly. I'm not sure you need to know either."

"What do you mean, you don't know exactly?"

Leonard doesn't intend to be rude. What does it mean when it's said that someone is a big character? In this case, it doesn't mean he is loud or talkative. A person who changes direction all the time comes across as uncertain. Leonard doesn't change direction; he is undeflectable; he picks an angle and doesn't stop until he reaches the edge of the paper. In truth his character is very much like everyone else's, with all the usual features – it's just this question of scale. And so whenever someone leans forward to take a closer look, as happens in routine social and professional exchanges like this one, what they see is an expanse of tough, impenetrable hide. The delicate eyelashes, the swishing tail, the whole comic outline – it takes time and perspective to understand that they are part of the picture too.

As is his habit, Leonard keeps going. "Are they busy, your Gatekeepers?"

"Only a few people on the top floor are cleared to know the answer to that question."

"What are the successes you mentioned?"

"That's irrelevant to our conversation. Listen —"

"How long has the programme existed for?"

"Now wait a damn minute," says Remnant.

He was warned about Leonard. Others are better *soft* interviewers, he was told – they make jokes, they smile and nod, they tack patiently towards the truth. But no one is a better *hard* interviewer than Leonard. That's what people say. Some spies are all about warmth, others are a blast of cold Arctic air. As the pre-eminent rat-catcher of his generation, a term bestowed upon him (behind his back) the day he won a confession from his seventh foreign agent in a year (an administrative assistant in the Passport Office recruited by the Iranians during a visit to his maternal grandmother in Esfahan), Leonard is squarely in the Arctic camp. Remnant is unsure how to proceed. Like a child he simply blurts out what he wants to be true.

"I'm in charge here. All these questions." He recalls that being a spy is about persuading people to do things, not ordering them. "Curiosity can't be switched off, can it? Like modern cars, the bloody headlights are always on. No doubt that's one of the things that makes you so good at your job, Leonard," he says, smiling foolishly. "Which is what has prompted this invitation. That and your Russian expertise, and of course the fact that you've met her at least once."

"Met who?"

"Willa Karlsson. But let's take a step backwards, get to know each other, shall we? Why don't you tell me about yourself? Does anyone call you Len or Lenny?"

2

At first glance, and most definitely before you get to know him, you might assume Leonard is a collector of something obscurely antiquated, or a young librarian from Hull, or even a clergyman (an impression encouraged by his adoption of a uniform of sorts: buffed brown derby shoes, white Oxford shirt, medium-wale tan corduroy jacket and trousers). Thin, bespectacled, bald on top and with a careless attitude to the stuff at the sides that in some neighbourhoods of East London makes him look more avant-garde than he intends. When at his most dangerous – poised to offend, to alarm, to intimidate – he stands at the angle of a lamp post hit by a slow-moving car. His fingers are long and delicate like those of a pianist or a surgeon, if there is such a thing as a pianist who only plays in a minor key, a surgeon whose only tool is the scalpel.

What might *explain* Leonard? As a child he was subject to periods of intense bullying at a series of provincial schools across Yorkshire, Lancashire and the Midlands. He idolized his father, who left when he was ten and didn't come back. For a few years after that, Leonard was convinced he could speak to animals. He developed a stutter. His mother struggled financially with four children, and he and his sisters all worked at least two part-time jobs from the age of fifteen onwards. Whatever narrow portion of happiness he claimed during those years was the result of a hard-fought negotiation with himself and the world around him. I'll be like *this* if I don't have to be like *that*. I'll make *this* concession but there's no way I'll give up *that*. The result is an unusual character. He now thinks of his childhood as the finely calibrated barrel of a gun that twisted him, that exerted huge pressure on him, that made him hurtle at breakneck speed not just to get away from *there*, but to get away from the next place as well, and the one after that. He abandoned a promising physics degree at Leeds University to take up a position editing the letters page of a minor literary magazine, before spending six months as an apprentice tailor in Cambridge and three years as a tutor in St Petersburg. In the gaps he refurbished classic cars, acquired three languages and – most taxing of all – bluffed his way through two summers as a sommelier in a four-rosette restaurant deep in the Suffolk countryside.

Generally speaking, this was how he expected to spend the rest of his life. Drift was as comforting to him as dry land was to others; in a different era he might have signed on as a merchant seaman. He had no interest in the idea that he should be defined by a job, and he had left any notion of social embarrassment in the claustrophobic care of his three deeply conventional sisters. Leonard liked variety, he liked novelty, he liked change. At twenty-one he'd unexpectedly inherited enough from his paternal grandmother to ensure he'd stay afloat as long as he did a spot of paddling from time to time, and it was in this spirit that a few months before his thirtieth birthday, in the autumn of 2010, he completed an online application form for a position with British intelligence.

His plan, insofar as there was a plan, was to stay for a year or two, or until he got bored; he already had one eye on a job planting trees on an island off the East Coast of America. In any case, he had low expectations of getting through the opaque recruitment process. It wasn't a question of lacking confidence in himself and his abilities – that has *never* been Leonard's problem. And he knew that in this day and age a Yorkshire accent and state school education wouldn't be held against him, even in the famously cloistered world of British intelligence. No, the problem he expected to encounter was the security clearance. The problem was the vetting.

It didn't occur to him to lie. The interview had taken so long to arrange that he was already more than halfway through finalizing arrangements for the job in America, and it would have been antithetical to his approach to life, now he felt free, to constrain himself voluntarily within a framework of untruths that would have to be maintained. So when the woman from Vetting pressed on his doorbell, he told her briskly and with one eye on his watch that during periods in his life he had been promiscuous, that she should write down in her notebook that this included a teenage sexual encounter on a cross-channel ferry with a man whose name he didn't know, that he'd once slashed the tyres of a teacher who told his sister she was stupid, that he saw nothing wrong with smoking marijuana but had never much liked the taste, and that over the years he had both won and lost considerable sums of money at the poker table.

"That's very interesting," she said. "Is poker really gambling? I'm told it's more about skill than luck."

"Not if you're blind drunk it's not. Then it's luck all the way."

He was surprised to be offered a job. He put it down to his bracing honesty and the office's interest in recruiting candidates from every conceivable background. In due course it occurred to him that the woman from Vetting might have discerned a quality in him he hadn't been aware of himself, because from the second he joined he loved it. Looking back, he wondered whether his life really had been aimless up to that point, or whether it had merely been the wobble that happens when an arrow first leaves the bow, because from his first day onwards he felt that he was flying straight and true and unswervingly into the heart of his country's enemies. He wouldn't have been embarrassed by such old-fashioned language. He flourished in an environment in which bad people did evil things – in which assassins murdered defectors, in which hackers stole secrets, in which deluded teenagers stabbed passers-by. He threw himself into the job with a Pauline zeal that was noted by his peers. After an early training exercise in which he left a role player in tears, Leonard's instructors wrote in their feedback that he displayed "an impressive ability to kneel on the bruise" and judged that he was "deployable on operations where the personal qualities required are independence, robustness and sheer bloody-minded persistence". "Thuggish ... despite appearances," they wrote. "Most definitely not a charmer."

It might well have been this quality that made the woman from Vetting overlook his shortcomings. She had introduced herself as Molly. It was only after he joined that he found out her real name was Willa.

3

"From our perspective in Gatekeeping, the last few years have been turbulent," says Charles Remnant. "We're not talking Cambridge Spy Ring turbulence, enough to ground an entire squadron. But we are talking headaches and nosebleeds in the cheap seats and – more importantly – up the road in first class."

The sound of footsteps outside. Remnant waits a full thirty seconds before continuing in a lower voice.

"You'll be aware that several years ago the father of an analyst called Jonas Worth was kidnapped in Syria. Linked to that was the theft of a large number of sensitive documents. We still don't know how many were taken or where they are now." He shoots his cuffs. Scars form a tangled nest around the gleaming blue of his glass eye. "More recent still is the case of August Drummond," he says. "He started to misbehave – if that's not too mild a word – almost as soon as he joined, meaning that we endured five years of misconduct, leaks and betrayal before my team caught him. We still don't understand his motives, or whether a dozen more things he's responsible for are yet to come to light."

"The Robin Hood case," says Leonard.

Remnant struggles to contain his irritation. "I'd prefer it if you didn't use that term," he says.

"That's what people call it, the Robin Hood case. Whether you like it or not. Where is he now?"

"Drummond? He turned up in Istanbul causing all sorts of trouble. Last I heard he'd broken his leg jumping off a rooftop on New Year's Eve. Drunk, I expect. Bloody fool. I wish it had been his neck."

"I'd be happy to speak to him for you," says Leonard. "I might be able to get some answers."

"I've heard about your ability to get answers. That's another reason you're sitting here – that whole 'rat-catcher' thing. But this is not about August Drummond or Jonas Worth. My point is simply that both cases involved catastrophic breakdowns in discipline and caused huge damage, internally and externally. The Americans are aware of the Worth case because they were involved in our efforts to contain him. And the very public nature of Drummond's actions, along with that wretched 'Robin Hood' term everyone seems to insist on using, means there's not a pot washer or dinner lady in this building who hasn't heard of him. There are other cases too – not many, single digits, but enough to make us worry that something is shifting under our feet. Cases involving disobedience, minor leaks, a refusal to obey orders."

Footsteps again, along with laughter. Remnant reacts as though his credibility has been challenged, as though someone has overheard his words and found them ridiculous. His face reddens.

"It's serious, damn serious. Just yesterday I briefed the DG about an archivist who has been behaving suspiciously," he says. "An archivist, do you hear, someone with access to thousands of our most sensitive files. Can you imagine the damage he could do if he mislaid or sold or heaven forbid *published* them? And yet the DG asks me to proceed with a light touch."

The laughter slows, settles into conversation. They listen in silence to an account of a night out at the weekend that ended with someone called Penny cheating on her boyfriend, who is called Martin. Although it isn't clear whether Penny or Martin even work in the office, Remnant tilts his head and makes a note in the corner of his pad. Leonard briefly admires him. He admires anyone without an off-switch. He remembers the one operation he ran alongside August Drummond, against a visiting Russian businessman with links to the Kremlin, and the way August swooped down mid-stride to pick up a rain-soaked business card from the gutter outside the Connaught, only to read it, smile and slip it into his jacket pocket. "You never know when a contact in that line of work might be useful," August murmured by way of explanation, and in that moment Leonard learned something about professional curiosity that he has never forgotten.

"Private Office has approved two measures in response to this … crisis," says Remnant. "The first is to bolster the well-being offer to staff. This means making sure everyone knows they can raise concerns in a safe, sympathetic environment and providing support for those dealing with personal or professional difficulties."

It's clear he finds talk of well-being uncomfortable. The ideas behind it are so alien he can't describe them in his own words. Instead he has swallowed the official language whole and now regurgitates it on demand.

"I saw a notice the other day inviting staff to attend a 'lethal strike drop-in'," says Leonard.

"What's your point?"

"Just that the office can sometimes tie itself in knots trying to be a modern, sympathetic employer. It can forget what it's here for." He waves a dismissive hand and leans forward, keen for Remnant to get to the point of all this. "You said Private Office has approved two measures. I assume the second is the Gatekeepers. Another reason to keep us secret."

"What do you mean?"

"Only that it jars with the first measure," says Leonard. "We want you to feel loved and looked after. But in case you don't, we've asked the person at the next desk to keep an eye on you."

"Wait a minute —"

"It's not a criticism. The only important thing is the work. Nothing must be allowed to get in the way of the work."

"We're harnessing an untapped resource, Leonard. Instead of pointing our most talented officers outwards like antennae towards the threat of terrorism and espionage, we remind them that there are threats walking around this very building – in the queue for coffee, lifting weights in the gym. Suspect everyone, we tell them. Then come back and share your darkest and most paranoid thoughts with us."

"It works, does it?"

"The way we caught August Drummond was by adopting a technique first used by the CIA to catch the Russian spy Aldrich Ames," says Remnant. "They had over a hundred suspects. To whittle that list down, they gave it to ten highly trusted officers and asked them to pick five individuals they thought might be a traitor, relying on nothing but professional instinct. All ten officers picked Ames. We did the same with Drummond. The results weren't quite so clear-cut, and in fact another name came top of the list, but the needle certainly flickered in his direction. We put a little pressure on him, he attacked one of my officers and the case fell open."

"You said this is about Willa. Was her name top of that list?"

"You're as exhausting as they say, Leonard." Remnant looks at his watch. "We'll come to what Willa may or may not have done in a moment. Before that, why don't you tell me what you thought of her?"

4

It was hard to form an impression during a conversation that was by its very nature one-way. Over the course of five hours, Willa asked Leonard about his current and historical debts, his friends and family, what it took to make him lose his temper, the cities and towns in Russia he had visited, how much he spent on alcohol in an average week, whether he had attended political marches, and much more besides. In her mannerisms Willa was such a distillation of vagueness, uncertainty and absent-mindedness that it had the effect of giving her character a kind of clear intensity. One of her pink woollen socks was pulled up to knee height while the other bunched slackly around her ankle, and her voluminous blue skirt was stained with egg yolk. There was a warm and attractive face beneath her smudged glasses, but it was often obscured by sighs, grimaces and shakes of the head. Life for Molly, as she called herself, was an endless series of small frustrations – with pens that leaked, with tissues that couldn't be coaxed out of sleeves.

When she went to the toilet Leonard picked up her notebook and read:

Candidate watches pornography on average once a week. Material viewed is heterosexual and mainstream. He does not purchase access to material or have accounts in his or any other name. He has never viewed material featuring real or staged violence, coercion, underage participants or bestiality.

Candidate drinks alcohol on average three times a week and consumes between five and eight units on each occasion.

On another page he saw:

> *Onions (red)*
> *Chicken stock*
> *Gravy granules*
> *Shoelaces*
> *Pork chop x 2*

Folded between the back pages of her notebook was a quick crossword from a tabloid newspaper; the clue to the only answer filled in was "entrance to room (4)". And the thought that flitted briefly across Leonard's mind that night, just before he fell asleep, was that Molly herself was a bit too much like a quick crossword, intended by its creator to be understood at a glance and scribbled over with words such as "eccentric" and "crazy" and "harmless" – an observation he put down to spies simply being spies.

"Willa has been in a medically induced coma since being admitted to hospital a month or so ago," says Remnant. "Her doctors suspect she has been the victim of a poisoning, chiefly because of the suddenness, complexity and severity of her symptoms, but they have been unable to identify any known toxins or chemicals in her system. Repeated examinations of her flat by experts have failed to come up with anything. If she was poisoned, therefore, it is likely to have been by a state actor, given the challenges involved in creating and delivering a poison we cannot detect."

He surveys his possessions, laid out in front of him on the table, and adjusts their formation, moving his pencil a fraction to one side while on the other flank a plain brown envelope with Leonard's name written on it advances three inches.

"Thoughts turn to Moscow when state-sponsored assassinations are discussed. But we all agree this is not a plausible theory. Killing a Russian defector is one thing. Killing a British intelligence officer, albeit one who retired a year ago, would be unprecedented. And let's not forget what Willa was – a vetting officer who had nothing whatsoever to do with Russian work. Vetting is essentially a function of HR. She had access to some staff data, this is true, but not to the wider intelligence work that is our bread and butter.

"By any measure her career was uneventful. When she joined more than thirty years ago she was briefly thought to be a rising star, but her file shows that she requested the move to the vetting department soon after and stayed there until her retirement last year. She was reasonably diligent, but far from being the most dynamic, curious, intelligent or ambitious member of her team. She never sought promotion, her appraisal markings were mediocre at best. No one remembers her ever asking suspiciously pointed questions." Remnant shakes his head. He looks tired. "There is simply no conceivable reason why the Russians would try to kill her. This was our position, and we have spent a good deal of time, energy and political capital reassuring the police and the Home Secretary that there was nothing here to concern them."

This was our position. Leonard hears the change in tense. He leans forward.

"On Friday a GCHQ outpost picked up a fragment of chatter between two Russian SVR officers," says Remnant, "one of whom referred in cryptic terms to an English oak being chopped down. It made no sense in the broader conversation, only as a code of some kind. Remember the wider context, Leonard – remember Jonas Worth, remember August Drummond. One more scandal will harm our reputation in ways that will take a generation or more to heal. And reputation is *everything* in this game. Reputation is the reason our friends work with us, but it's also the reason our enemies keep their distance. Without reputation, London will be just another playground for the Russians – another Brussels, another Vienna.

"For this reason we have taken the difficult decision *not* to inform Whitehall about the latest Russian intelligence.

Before we do that we want to get a full assessment of the situation, but in the most discreet way possible. Which is where you come in. You are going to find out for us within the next two weeks whether there's anything at all in Willa Karlsson's life that has even the slightest stink of Russia."

The word "mission" is never used: it is too dramatic, too religious, too *American*. But this is precisely how Leonard feels about the task he is being given. To shine a light into the darkness, to sacrifice himself for a greater cause – he will do whatever it takes. Leonard feels he was created from dust for moments like this.

"You have been chosen because you know the Russian subject well enough to recognize the signs if you see them," says Remnant. "More importantly, you've been chosen because we want answers, not some wishy-washy fudge of an investigation after which we're none the wiser. We want you to stick out those famously pointed elbows and get to the bottom of this, Leonard. If there's something to be found, find it. If there's nothing to be found, convince me you have turned over every conceivable stone. You have two weeks from today. Is that clear?"

"The worst possible scenario is that Willa was a Russian agent, something went wrong and they tried to kill her to cover their tracks," says Leonard. "Is that what you're asking me to do – to find out if she was a Russian agent?"

"Yes."

"She fell ill a month ago. You haven't been sitting on your hands all this time. What have you found?"

"Nothing of any value. Bear in mind that because of the sensitivity of this subject we have been unable to deploy the traditional battery of resources. No more than six people in this building are aware of this. We've had one analyst looking at data – at Willa's phone records, travel, medical history, known associates. But what are we looking for exactly? She didn't have a mobile phone, she didn't use email, she preferred cash. She hasn't been out of the country in the last ten years. It's like trying to spot a shipwreck hundreds of feet beneath a choppy sea. The only way to get answers is to drop someone down to carry out a fingertip search of the ocean floor, and that someone is you. What are you working on now?"

"Oligarchs."

"Anything that can't be paused for two weeks?"

"No."

"Put in a request for leave. Your manager doesn't know anything about this. The other reason we've chosen you is that you've met Willa, which will come in useful as we've told the police that according to our personnel records you're her long-lost nephew. They'll give you access to her flat. Have a nose around, but don't make too much noise or smash anything up as there's a neighbour downstairs with sensitive ears. Create a suitable legend for yourself: a boring job, family circumstances, a home far away from here. We've allocated a central London property for you to use as a base. Here are the keys and several sets of alias documents, including one with a Karlsson surname, in case that comes in handy. I suggest you start immediately: the clock is —"

Leonard stands up so quickly that his chair rolls back and hits the wall with a loud crash.

FROM THE ARCHIVES

1A

CONFIDENTIAL

15 July 2018

Dear Director,

After much careful consideration, having recently completed my 34th year in this office, I have for personal reasons and with a heavy heart made the difficult decision to tender my resignation, with immediate effect.

I cannot begin to convey the enormous pride I have taken in my work over the years, and the satisfaction in seeing a much-changed organization from the one I joined in 1984.

Please know that whatever the future holds, I will be cheering you on wholeheartedly from the sidelines.

Yours sincerely

Willa Karlsson

CONFIDENTIAL

1B

SUBJECT: HIT Training Report (Leonard FLOOD)
DATE: 15 October 2012

1. Leonard performed to a high standard on the recent Human Intelligence and Tradecraft (HIT) course and we are pleased to certify him as fit and ready for operational duties.

2. In addition to his language abilities and varied professional experiences prior to joining the office, Leonard brings a unique set of personal qualities and characteristics to his work. Notable among these are a single-minded focus on the task ahead of him, a determination to exceed objectives and an impressively agile mind. His recall of detail is strong and his written reports demonstrate clarity of thought and an awareness – most of the time – of his personal shortcomings.

3. Leonard demonstrated particular ability in the Intelligence Interviewing module. His preparation for each role play was extremely thorough and he adapted the techniques

we teach in imaginative and unexpected ways. In the live exercise phase, more than one role player commented on the fact that they disclosed more information to Leonard than they had intended ("I realized afterwards I'd told him everything instead of holding a few things back as per the brief"). He projects gravitas and is able to leverage this to pressure interviewees into making full disclosure ("He just sits and waits for you to answer", "It's like all the air suddenly goes out of the room"). Indeed, Leonard displayed an impressive ability to kneel on the bruise and extract every last detail from his subjects, even in situations where sympathy and kindness would arguably have been a better tactical choice. As one of the role players commented afterwards, it is not always necessary to leave an interviewee feeling squeezed completely dry, particularly if there may be some advantage to recruiting them as a long-term agent ("I told him everything but I never want to see him again").

4. Leonard will benefit from ongoing development in the areas of ingratiation and projecting warmth. He will need to become more aware of the intensity of his manner, which is at times highly effective and at other times deeply off-putting. ("He's definitely not the sort of person you'd strike up a conversation with in a bar.") He can be thuggish in his approach despite appearances and is most definitely not a charmer. He is solitary by nature and did not integrate particularly well with his fellow students. Our usual experience is that we have to remind at least one student per course that they should take training more seriously. Our experience with Leonard, however, was the opposite: more than once he had to be told that in this environment

we actively encourage students to relax, enjoy themselves and accept that they will make mistakes in the broader interest of their learning.

5. Nevertheless, we judge that Leonard has the potential to develop into a formidable field officer if developed with care and used correctly. We recommend that at this early stage in his career he is not selected for operations requiring the ability to build rapport. He is, however, deployable on operations where the personal qualities required are independence, robustness and sheer bloody-minded persistence. He also has the attributes required to be an extremely effective interviewer. We have in mind some of the more skilful, evasive and hostile targets encountered in this job. Many of them will not see him coming. Even police undercover officers with decades of experience who role-played on the course found it difficult to develop an effective strategy against Leonard. ("When he walked in the room, I thought, 'Hello vicar. We're going to have some fun with you.' But when he walked out at the end, I turned to Tommy and said, 'What the fuck just happened?'") This ability should not be underestimated. We do not see it very often. If Leonard learns to control the impression he makes on others, to vary his intensity and foreground the softer skills he undoubtedly does possess, he will grow into a versatile, stealthy and highly effective operational officer.

6. We look forward to seeing Leonard in one year for his annual tradecraft refresher.

1C

SUBJECT: Re: Nominations for Queen's Honours
DATE: 10 January 2019

Dear Felicity,

Further to your kind bulletin inviting staff to submit the names
of colleagues deserving of a place on this year's Queen's
Honours List, I am writing once again to propose the name
of Charles Remnant.

Charles joined the Service in 1989 at the age of twenty-nine
after six years in the British Army that saw operational tours
in Northern Ireland and the Falklands. He suffered a setback
early in his career with us when he was brutally attacked and
blinded in one eye by an undercover Iraqi intelligence officer. It
was later discovered that the Iraqi had been responsible for the
murder of numerous opponents of Saddam Hussein's regime
who had sought refuge in the United Kingdom.

Charles bore his affliction courageously, taking the decision
to leave operational work and move into the Gatekeeping team,

where he has remained for over twenty years as a champion of robust investigations into those "that would with treason wound this fair land's peace", as the Bard of Avon so eloquently puts it. A standard-bearer for probity in public life, Charles has been at the helm of investigations into a number of convicted foreign agents, including a parliamentary researcher, the CFO of a leading arms manufacturer and a Royal Navy submariner. Most recently, Charles has spearheaded operations against two members of this Service, one who is believed to have stolen a cache of sensitive documents and the other who waged an insidious campaign of disobedience over the six years of his employment. In the former operation I had the honour of acting as Charles's field man, and I can testify to his tireless determination to pursue and punish those who would betray their country.

In his personal life, Charles is a church warden, an enthusiastic beekeeper, a devoted husband to Betsy and secretary of his club's membership committee – no doubt the most rigorous and demanding holder of that position in their long history!

In years gone by, Felicity, I have stopped at this point in my exhortations. However, the unfortunate truth, as we both know, is that all previous attempts to nominate Charles have been unsuccessful. For this reason, and to avoid yet another disappointment, I would like to "bite the bullet" and address some possible misapprehensions about my dear friend that might be acting as an obstacle to a long-overdue honour. I am aided in this endeavour by the existence of documentary evidence of the lies concerning Charles that may currently be in circulation.

In his first foray onto one of the office's online "staff chat rooms" several years ago, Charles's unfamiliarity with the technology led to him making a number of comments that he quickly retracted but that some felt were dismissive of modern phenomena like anxiety, depression and stress. His words provoked a barrage of ad hominem attacks, including the accusation that Charles takes pleasure in firing officers on scant evidence; that he is Pharisaical in his adherence to the letter of the law; that he does not believe in affording others the benefit of the doubt; and that he displays total indifference towards the way that the personal circumstances of an individual might impact upon their professional conduct. Many of these attacks were also retracted. But they have left behind a cloud of gun smoke that lingers several years on. Most egregious of all was the utterly fallacious smear that Charles has used the unique influence afforded to him by his position to undermine political rivals and extend what has been an unprecedented tenure in the role of Head of Gatekeeping.

My calm and measured response to all this, Felicity, beyond asserting that it is categorically untrue, is to point out, strictly inter nos, that Charles suffered considerably in the months and years after being partially blinded by the Iraqi officer, and that one of the ways he has "processed" that appalling incident is by being particularly zealous in his pursuit of traitors. Good for him, I say. My less measured response to these accusations is that any Head of Gatekeeping who succeeds in being popular is simply not doing his (or possibly even her) job.

Yours sincerely

Desmond Naseby

CHAPTER TWO

Monday, 1225

The first thing that occurs to Leonard as he opens the door to Willa's flat is that it looks uninhabited. A long corridor stretches away from him: exposed pine floorboards, empty white walls, two naked light bulbs, a high ceiling edged with cornicing. The only sign of life is a thin overcoat hanging from a hook on his left. A single hook: this isn't a home that sees many visitors.

He carries her post through to the small living room at the end of the corridor. The flat is on the top floor of a Victorian house converted into a jumble of twelve units, and treetops stretch in every direction like dense green clouds punctured only by the needle-sharp spires of suburban churches. He opens a window to let in some air. The world outside is painted in the bright, happy colours of a child. He looks through the post, registering the fact that in the month Willa has been in hospital there has been no personal correspondence from a friend or relative, only circulars from charities, an estate agent's valuation of the flat and an advertisement from a local cleaning service. Her latest bank statement tells him very little.

Leonard considers what he is looking for. He has searched several properties belonging to Russian agents, some under cover of darkness, others in broad daylight after the police had come and gone, taking with them anything that looked like evidence. Willa fell ill suddenly, he thinks, so she won't have had the opportunity to prepare for a search. If there's something to be found, it will be in its usual hiding place – or even in plain sight. In one Mayfair townhouse, the only thing he found over five floors was a single vinyl record of Cossack folk songs inside the sleeve of a Beethoven symphony; on another occasion it was a collection of phone chargers in the back of a sock drawer but only one phone. The signs can sometimes be more obvious: dozens of SIM cards, inexplicable amounts of cash, a piece of communications equipment disguised as an everyday electrical object, even stolen documents. Being an agent is stressful, so Leonard knows to be on the lookout for drugs, medication, pornography, large amounts of alcohol or evidence of gambling.

He measures each room and draws a floor plan. For an old property, even one that might be expected to warp and bend and buckle over time, the measurements add up, suggesting there are no obvious concealments built into the walls. He starts in the bathroom, checking the toilet cistern and taking apart the flush mechanism. Then he removes the bath panel and examines the space underneath, finding only a dirty rag and roll of duct tape left by the builder. He shines a torch down the drains. There's no prescription medicine in the cabinet above the sink, only a selection of toiletries and make-up. He opens the window and leans out to look for anything hanging down against the external wall or behind the drainpipe. There are no loose floor tiles.

In the bedroom he removes each item of clothing from the wardrobe and runs his fingers along the seams. He finds an Oyster card in the pocket of a shirt. Willa's clothes are simple in colour and style but clean and cared-for: there are mothballs in two of the drawers and the labels of many of the items have been pricked by tiny holes that suggest a dry-cleaner's safety pin. There is a small pile of books on the bedside table: a collection of Carol Ann Duffy poems, a Georges Simenon paperback and a worn, cloth-covered field guide for birdwatchers in the British Isles. None of the poems have been annotated, none of the pages have been torn out, none of the corners have been folded. He can't coax the novel to fall open consistently at the same page. Notes have been scribbled on a handful of pages in the field guide and he puts it to one side for examination later. A single bookshelf on the wall holds a small collection that includes Sylvia Plath, C. S. Lewis, Wilfred Owen, Tolstoy and an anthology of Nietzsche's political writing. There is nothing under the bed or in the bed frame, and he spends close to twenty-five minutes examining the mattress for signs that the stitching has ever been loosened.

The living room and kitchen take another hour. In a drawer he finds a passport, National Insurance card, household bills, spare keys and a handful of photographs, the most recent of which was taken at least ten years ago. Apart from childhood pictures of Willa as a young girl with what appear to be various relatives, the rest look as though they were taken on holiday in different parts of rural England. The only stamp in her passport is from a visit to America in 2008. Leonard crumbles a half-eaten block of Norfolk fudge into pieces and empties and refills every box of pasta, rice and lentils. All the liquids go down the sink.

Finally he empties her handbag onto the table: a purse containing £33.61 and a local supermarket receipt dated the day before she collapsed, a single debit card, another Oyster card, her driving licence, a tube of lipstick and a set of house keys. He sits down and contemplates the results of his labour. In a little under four hours he has found nothing suspicious, nothing inexplicable, nothing expensive or Russian or concealed or remotely suggestive of espionage, nothing more technical than a hairdryer he breaks into dozens of pieces.

He goes back to where he started, wondering what he has missed. The corridor walls are chalky with expensive paint, the light cables braided from dark red fabric. He goes into her bedroom and in the absence of a better idea takes off his jacket and trousers and puts on one of her dresses. He wasn't expecting to do this today. But the momentum that drives Leonard through life is present also in his sense of who he is. Within the boundaries of what is possible, he believes, freedom must be exercised, like a prisoner taking his laps of the yard. He slips Willa's coat over the dress. It is a good fit. Two brightly coloured cloth bags are bundled into the left pocket. He looks at himself in the mirror, allowing his thoughts to settle, allowing a vague outline to appear – one that to his surprise doesn't contradict Remnant's suspicions. This is what he thinks: the orderliness of Willa's living environment is at odds with the chaotic physical appearance she presented in person. There are no leaking pens in this flat, no stray tissues abandoned in sleeves. The only tissue is in the right-hand pocket of her coat, a coat that exists to be shrugged on as a disguise to protect her against the outside world. Her book collection suggests intelligence and a willingness to engage with complexity, which is very different to the impression Willa's colleagues have formed of her. Why did she keep her true character hidden? Where are the rest of her books? Is it possible that the only philosopher she read was Nietzsche, that someone who enjoyed *romans durs* hadn't got through numerous other novels on the way? And these cloth bags with their bright colours – it's important to her that the bags are noticed. Most people only have the capacity to remember one thing about a person, and Leonard wonders whether at some point Willa calculated that the sight of a grey-haired woman carrying bags would comfortably fill that space. People would look no further. The bags are part of her disguise.

Leonard is a spycatcher by training, experience and instinct; he knows better than anyone that it is possible to spend years watching a target and come to no firm conclusion about what they are doing. But in the case of Willa Karlsson, considering he has been working on it for a matter of hours, he feels overwhelmed with leads. His realization that she is in the habit of hiding things is as significant in its own small way as the discovery of a stolen file beneath the floorboards.

He packs a selection of her books into his rucksack and considers what to do next. The birdwatching guide reminds him of a time when he wanted to earn pocket money beating for a local landowner's shoot. He has never forgotten the instructions given by a laconic Yorkshire gamekeeper on the first day: cover ground, make noise, don't let up. It was a period in his childhood when Leonard was at his most unhappy, and he felt so protective towards the birds that as soon as he was out of sight he took off his boots to avoid disturbing them. He didn't mind that the ground tore at his feet. When it became clear he wasn't saving any lives he charged out of the undergrowth at the shooting party waving his arms and shouting, but they laughed and cheered him on and swivelled their guns into the sky. He didn't cry once, even when the gamekeeper gave him a hard slap for good measure as he threw him out at the nearest gate, even when he had to walk the five miles home without his boots.

Cover ground, make noise, don't let up. If only Remnant had been so concise in his instructions.

Monday, 1620

THE DRY-CLEANER

"Crikey, it's warm out there," says Leonard. "Lovely and cool in here though."

"It's not corduroy weather, love, that's for sure. Says here it'll be mid-thirties tomorrow."

She gently slaps the tabloid; it sticks to her palm and lifts off the counter. Another woman works on a sewing machine in the back. She is bent low, her eye level with the flashing needle, as though the machine might cheat her out of a stitch if she were to take her eye off it for a moment.

"My aunt thinks she forgot to collect a coat," Leonard says.

"Got a ticket?"

"She was mugged last week and they took her handbag. She's fairly sure the ticket was in there, but between us her memory's a little foggy."

"I'm not surprised, poor love." She closes the paper and turns around. "Did you hear that, Doreen? Another mugging. Nearby, was it?"

"Walking home from the station. In broad daylight. Two teenagers waving a screwdriver."

"I can't remember the last time I saw a policeman around here. What's her name, your aunt?"

"Willa Karlsson." He takes out one of the photographs he found in the drawer. He doesn't care about the coat but wants them to know who he's talking about. "I've got a picture of the one she thinks she dropped off. In case that helps."

"Oh yes," she says. "Doreen, it's that lady from round the corner, the one with all the bags. I'm pretty sure we haven't got that coat though. Cashmere, is it? Could she have taken it somewhere else?"

"This is her regular place. She always says how nice you are to her. How often does she pop in?"

"Every other week, I'd say. But we haven't seen her for a little while."

"You haven't got anything else under her name, have you?"

She runs her finger down the columns in a book and shakes her head. "I'm sorry, dear – nothing else."

"I'm stumped then. She couldn't have had a friend drop it off for her, could she? Is it under someone else's name?"

"Anything's possible, dear. But we'd need a ticket."

"Did you ever see her in here with anyone else? Any local friends? I hate to go on about it but she's lost a brooch, a family heirloom. It belonged to her grand-mother. But she can't remember for the life of her whether it was in the coat or the handbag. With everything that's happened she's just so upset that I'm struggling to get much sense out of her."

"She's lucky to have someone like you looking out for her." She reaches out to pat his hand. "I only ever see my nephew when he wants something. If we'd found a brooch we'd have given her a call. I never saw her with anyone else. Doreen, did you ever see her with anyone? No, she was always on her own. Let me have another look for you." She returns to the book. "The last thing she brought in was two shirts. That was six weeks ago, and she collected them both. I wish we could help."

"Chances are she left the coat somewhere local then – a shop or a cafe or something like that."

"Most likely."

He goes to the window and looks out at the street. "At least she's not going to need it in this weather." The arcade opposite includes a bookmaker, a charity shop and a boarded-up cheesemonger. "Where do you think I should start? Did you ever see her in any other places?"

"Doreen, didn't you say you saw her getting her hair done in that place by the church? I only remember it because her hair's normally such a bird's nest, no offence meant." The door opens and a man comes in pushing a toddler in a pram. "Oh, hello there Mr Davenport, come for your suit, have you?" Turning back to Leonard, she says, "Give your aunt our best." She lowers her voice to a whisper. "Tell her I'll do her first item half price when she's back on her feet. I'm sure Doreen won't mind me saying that."

"I'd like to book a haircut for my aunt," says Leonard.

"Of course." The manager picks up a tablet and stabs at the screen accusingly. "When do you want to book her in for?"

"She's in hospital at the moment, so I was wondering if you could send someone to her. Is that possible? The hospital said it'd be fine. I'm happy to pay whatever it takes. She's unwell and I know it'd lift her spirits."

"We can certainly do that. Do you know who normally cuts her hair?"

"Could you check for me? My aunt's name is Willa Karlsson."

"Let me have a look." She taps the screen. "Samantha's done her the last few times."

"Is Samantha here today?"

"She went for a break." The manager looks out of the window but can't locate her. Her mouth twists with irritation. "When are you thinking of?"

"How about next Wednesday morning at ten? I'll check that suits her and call you in a bit to confirm."

Samantha is easy enough to find. No more than twenty-five, halfway through her second cigarette, scissored into a gap on the pavement between a bollard and a bin that provides her with cover from her boss's line of sight. Her phone wobbles on the plinth of one bony knee.

"Are you Samantha?" Leonard says. "I just spoke to your boss about a haircut for my aunt." He glances back at the window. "She seems a bit of a dragon, your boss."

"One way to put it." She squints at him and holds up her cigarette. "Yeah, is it okay, I'm just having —"

"My aunt's in hospital and I want to arrange something nice to lift her spirits. She told me she really likes the way you cut it. She said you've got the magic touch."

"Look, actually, mate, if you don't mind, I've only got five —"

"What'd really cheer her up is a new hairstyle. I've got this picture of her from a few years ago." Leonard realizes her main worry is that him standing there will blow her cover. He squats down. "Do you think you could do it like this?"

"Oh, it's her, is it?" She takes the photograph. "This must have been a few years ago, she doesn't wear it like that now."

"I'm happy to pay over the odds. A big tip for you too, given the hassle of going all the way to the hospital."

"Oh yeah? When you say big…"

"Twenty quid. Think you could do it?"

"Doesn't she live on the road by the station, your aunt? A customer told me the police have been round there, all hush-hush. Wearing their white suits like on the telly."

"Looking for fingerprints. There's a gang targeting vulnerable elderly people."

She gets up.

Leonard stands between her and the salon. "I'm trying to work out if there's anything else I can do to lift her spirits," he says, "but I haven't seen her for a couple of years."

"I'm sure a haircut will help." She looks over his shoulder. "Listen, mate, I've really —"

"Do you know if she had any local friends? Anyone who I could ask to visit her in hospital?"

She shrugs.

"Was she chatty? Did she ever mention anyone? I can imagine for someone lonely like her she must have appreciated having a friendly person like you to talk to."

"To be honest it was mostly telly, the weather, that sort of thing."

"My mum suggested we get her a weekend away in a hotel somewhere as a treat. Do you know if she had any favourite places?"

"She had a bit of a tan once, I remember that. I told her it looked nice with her hair colour. Tried to persuade her to get some lowlights. But —"

"Do you know where she went?"

"To the countryside, that's all she said. We had a bit of a moan about young men who won't give up their seats."

"On trains?"

"Yeah. Look, I'd better get —"

"She didn't seem different or anything, the last time you saw her? Depressed or worried or anything?"

"Bloody hell, you're a bit full-on. You know, mate, I just cut her hair – I'm not her therapist or anything. I'm going to get into trouble, my boss is waving at me. Next appointment must have got here early. Don't forget about that tip, yeah? It's got to be cash or that bitch will keep it for herself."

"My aunt's asked me to drop this round for you," says Leonard. He holds up one of Willa's shirts. "It's in pretty good nick."

"Ooh, I like that colour. Very on-trend, your aunt." She's reading an orange Penguin paperback and has the outline of a Disney character tattooed on her upper arm. "That's really sweet of her. I'm sure we'll sell it on quickly."

"Ah, another northern accent. Makes me feel homesick."

"Where are you from?" she asks.

"I moved around a bit, but a few years near Blackpool, then over towards Leeds. What about you? Sunderland is my guess."

"Spot on. Most people say Newcastle."

"It's quite gentle though. Have you been down in London for a while?"

"Five years. I hope I'm not losing it."

"Who wants to sound like a southerner, right?"

"My mum would kill me." She picks up a clothes hanger and starts to unbutton the shirt. "We'll get this in the window today."

"I think my aunt probably does Gift Aid, if that helps."

"What's her name, I'll have a look."

"Willa Karlsson."

"Oh yes, we've got her details down here."

"I used to volunteer too. It all makes a difference, right?"

"It certainly does."

"What does she bring in? I'd wager half the books on your shelves are hers, given how much she reads."

She laughs. "It's people like your aunt that keep us going."

"Ah, that reminds me, it's a bit of a long shot but she said she's mislaid a receipt for an expensive watch. She uses them as bookmarks – receipts, that is, not expensive watches – and she wondered whether she might have left it in one of the ones she donated. Do you think that's possible? She'd come in herself only she's laid up in hospital at the moment."

"I don't think you'd find it now. One of the volunteers goes through the books before they put them on the shelves and they'd throw away something like a receipt."

"Are they up to date sorting the books?" He looks around for a storeroom. "When I was volunteering there was always a massive backlog waiting to be sorted. Never enough hours in the day, are there?"

"There are tonnes of books back there, you're right, but there's no way of knowing which ones come from your aunt, I'm really sorry."

"Do you mind if I have a quick peek?" He takes a half step towards the door in the corner. One way or another he's going in there, but he'd rather avoid returning after hours for something so speculative if he can help it. He's already been around the back for a look and the neighbouring shop is an off-licence with at least a couple of cameras. "I might spot something I recognize. It's a receipt for a Cartier watch, they're saying they won't fix it without proof of purchase. If I don't find it I'll leave you in peace, I promise."

She leads him into a room filled with cardboard boxes and unsorted clothes. Along one side is a long table listing under the weight of hundreds of books. "Let's see, here they are. What kind of things does she read? What are we looking for?"

"Poetry's her favourite. She's reading Carol Ann Duffy at the moment."

"Oh, I like her. 'Some nights I dreamed he'd written me', isn't that one of hers? Everything's jumbled up, they haven't been sorted yet. Poetry doesn't sell that well, so you might be in luck. Let's see, there's Yeats here, Wordsworth. This anthology is quite popular, we get a few of these through the shop."

"I think we can forget about these airport thrillers. Not her cup of tea. And all these sports biographies. Bloody hell, it's amazing how many footballers think their life deserves a four-hundred-page memoir. Who on earth is this fella?"

"That one sells like hot cakes."

He runs his finger down a dusty tower of books. "What about this lot?" he says. "Ted Hughes, here's a Larkin. All the best poets are northern, don't you think? We've got more soul than southerners."

"Larkin was born in Coventry," she says.

"I'd claim that as the north. And didn't he write his best poetry in, where was it, Sheffield?"

"Hull."

"You know your stuff. Some of these books are in mint condition. One careful lady owner, what do you think?"

"There's a Simon Armitage over here. What about this? Does she speak Russian, your aunt?"

"She's got hidden depths, has Aunt Willa, so it wouldn't surprise me. What else have you got? This is more her cup of tea, I've heard her talk about this French fella. Do you mind if I take a couple of these? I'll pay a fair price, don't worry."

"No problem. Any sign of that receipt?"

"Afraid not. Early days though. Maybe I'll have a look at —"

"Hang on, there's a customer out front. I'm really sorry, but you can't stay in here on your own."

THE CHURCH

"Father, have you got a minute?"

"What is it?"

Leonard has sat through the last ten minutes of a service attended by fewer than a dozen people. The church is as humid and airless as a swimming pool. The brick walls glow red in swampy evening sunlight that swells through the windows.

"My aunt is Willa Karlsson, she lives locally. She's been taken ill and I was wondering if I could arrange for someone to visit her in hospital."

"Ah, poor Willa – I'm so sorry to hear that. Can I ask what's wrong?" Sweat blackens his shirt at the armpits, around the paunch. The heat has soured him; already he's impatient to get away.

Leonard decides to draw this one out as long as he can. It's not just that the priest seems to know Willa; it's that Leonard is fond of churches. It is true of everything to some extent, but nothing more so than a church, that if you stand at one angle it is a place of profound beauty but if you take one step to either side it is utterly ridiculous. He likes this yearning quality churches have – he likes their *ambition*. It's what led him to religious faith for a full month during his turbulent adolescence.

"It's a number of things come all at once, Father. She had a tumble, and now she's suffering with blinding headaches. They're still trying to work out what it is. I'll be spending a bit of time down here with her, but I've got to go back up north in a few days and don't want her left all alone."

"And she's your aunt, you say." The priest cocks his head. "How's that?"

Leonard leans forward. He senses danger, he senses opportunity. That this priest knows her well enough to doubt the existence of a nephew. "Loosely speaking," he says. "My mother and her mother were distant cousins, but I was brought up to call Willa auntie. Not that she always appreciated it."

"Is that right?"

"You know her well, do you?" asks Leonard.

"Willa keeps to herself. But we've had a few good conversations over the years, and she pops in every now and then. I'm sorry to hear she's unwell. We'll remember her in our prayers on Sunday. The pastoral team organize visits to the sick and the elderly, so if you put her details in that box over there they'll deal with it in the morning." The sweat blackens his grey shirt like melting tar. He plucks at it with a grimace as though hot to the touch. There is a stained-glass image of a man carrying a cross ten feet away, but this priest can't get over his prickly heat.

"And Mass and confession?" asks Leonard.

"If she wants them, sure."

"I don't know how religious she is, that's why I ask. I don't mean to pry – I just want to make sure she has everything she needs. The truth is, Father, I feel guilty. I've lost touch with her in recent years. She was on holiday outside London when she fell, and I hate to think of her being all alone when something so distressing happened."

The priest examines Leonard. There is an unblinking, implacable quality to this odd-looking young man that unsettles him. He's used to being in charge but senses that on this occasion he's not, and he doesn't understand why or how, which makes him uncomfortable. He rummages for something worthless to get rid of his unwanted visitor. "God will look after her," he says. He must have dozens of such empty phrases to hand. Leonard doesn't move, so he adds, 'There's nothing to be gained by blaming yourself, young man."

"I suppose you're right," says Leonard. He turns his face towards the window and contemplates its image of patient suffering. He'd like to throw a rock through it. It wouldn't be the first time. It had been an unorthodox way to announce he was leaving the church. After only one month you'd think he'd stop going and that would be it. But his brief exposure to faith had opened up imaginary dimensions and layers of possible meaning, it had tried in its confused way to tell him he was loved, something he had never heard before, and he wanted to depart in a way that paid tribute to the dramatic richness of everything it had laid before him. The vicar had come running out and held him down and when the police arrived all Leonard was able to say by way of explanation for the broken window was that he didn't think Jesus would have wanted him to just slink away. "It's the thought of Willa lying there all alone waiting for help," he says. "It keeps me awake at night."

"She might have been visiting a friend."

"Is there anyone I should get in touch with, Father, anyone who knows her and might want to visit her in hospital?" asks Leonard.

"Why don't you leave that with me?"

"Do you know her friend outside London, the one she stayed with? Could I get in touch with … is it a he or a she?"

"I really can't help you, I'm afraid." The priest takes a long look at his watch. "If that's —"

"There is something else I wanted to raise with you, Father. If you don't mind me taking up so much of your time." Without waiting for an answer, Leonard sits in the nearest pew and waits for the priest to join him. He's fairly sure he's taken this as far as he can, but it isn't in his character to stop before the edge of anything. "Her doctors have suggested the problem may be psychological as well, that some kind of stress or pressure is contributing to her condition. She's only just started opening up about it. As I said, I've been so preoccupied with other things that I've neglected her. But I'm determined to help her recover."

"How admirable," he murmurs, sitting down reluctantly.

"I'd imagine this is something that's come up in your conversations. I don't know if she's a regular at confession, Father."

The priest makes a meaningless gesture.

"The thing is, she's really pretty unwell," says Leonard, "and from what I've been told by the professionals she's got to find a way to open up about this to continue the healing process. She's got to talk about it with someone. They've referred her to a psychologist, but I think her needs are spiritual as well. She's always been fond of C. S. Lewis. What was it he said, something about there being no peace without God?" The priest is quiet. Leonard might as well go all in, there's no point holding anything back now. "She's got a couple of Orthodox icons in her flat – I think they're from the Russian church – and I know how much sustenance she draws from them, and from her faith in general."

"I'm not sure I follow. What is it you think she needs to open up about?"

"She's hinted to me that she's got a … secret that's been eating away at her for a number of years now," he says. "It sounds dramatic, I know. But if we pool our resources then we stand a much better chance of —"

"What's your name?"

"David."

"David, let me stop you there. I'm quite busy today, and I'll admit I'm a little puzzled by all this. Whatever

Willa has or hasn't discussed with me is private. That's the first thing. The second thing is that I'm surprised to learn she has any kind of nephew, from what she's told me of her family, and in the course of my two visits to her flat I've never seen a Russian icon. It's entirely possible you're right and I just don't know her that well. But the best thing might be for you to leave her details in the wooden box over there and let the churchwardens deal with this in the morning. Would that be all right? Thank you so much for coming to see us."

There is something exhilarating about going too far. It feels like burning a house down. Leonard would justify it by saying that if you burn a house down you find out very quickly what a person values and where they hide it. But the truth is that he also likes burning things down.

"What were you doing in her flat, Father?" he asks.

"I think you'd better leave."

Monday, 2155

Leonard sits in darkness at Willa's kitchen table. He turns over the scraps of his afternoon's work: that she went to the countryside by train at least once; that she may have been visiting a friend; that no one can remember seeing her with another person; that she was friends of a sort with the priest; that she might be able to speak Russian.

It's more than he expected to find. The main value in doing the rounds of her neighbourhood was to accelerate himself into the pace required to meet Remnant's deadline, because to make progress in two weeks Leonard will have to abandon a spy's habit of cautious scepticism, of doubting everything, since that would result in him spending the entire time waiting for something better to come along. Instead he will have to act as though *everything* means *something*. And he is comfortable with this – he is comfortable drawing inferences from hints shaved off the hard edge of facts: that a target's decision to walk down this alleyway rather than that street means they have begun an anti-surveillance route, that a subtle shift in tone during a phone call indicates a cultivation is under way.

He is aware, too, how dangerous such thin judgements can be. He wonders how he will ever get away from that experience. It has defined his reputation in ways he knows are undeserved. The individual in question was a forty-six-year-old mid-ranking Russian civil servant named Aleksandr Baladin who walked into the British embassy in Brussels one blustery autumn afternoon, six years earlier, picked a leaf off his Burberry scarf and explained to the confused receptionist that he wished to speak with someone about a possible future outside Russia. The machinery ground into operation within the hour. First the confirmation that such a person existed and was in Brussels, then the assessment that he was positioned close enough to key figures in the Kremlin to provide intelligence of value.

But the priority at that early stage, before even thinking of accepting his offer, was to establish he wasn't a dangle intended to waste British time. There could be no worse outcome than to accept Baladin as a genuine defector only to see him board a plane back to a hero's welcome in Moscow six months later. Such an outcome would cripple morale. It would make everyone doubt their judgement and necessitate a painful review to establish what had been revealed of British strengths and weaknesses. Those officers who had been exposed to him would see their careers curtailed. The sheer deadening weight of wasted resources – security, assessment, validation, dissemination – would exhaust them all for years to come.

Leonard was dispatched. It was the first big case of his career. In the windowless basement of a townhouse near the embassy, with two analysts, a psychologist and a senior manager listening from the adjoining room, Leonard began to ask Baladin questions about his life. He started in English and switched to Russian after he'd heard the whole story twice. He went over the same facts repeatedly from different directions, making small changes to his questions each time. He knew that if Baladin was lying, his story would fray in visible ways. Watch his fingers, watch his feet – Leonard had learned that suppressed tension often showed itself at a person's extremities. He was so painstaking that the analysts began to work in shifts. His purpose in moving at such a pace was to tire the man out. He knew the Russians wouldn't have given Baladin a completely fake story to tell. It would be impossible to recount dozens of anecdotes about encounters, departments, characters, careers and arguments if they were all untrue – if there wasn't a real memory behind them of what this room had looked like or how that man had been dressed. If this was a dangle, the one element of his story that would sound a false note was the man's motive for defecting, and that was precisely where they began to run into difficulties.

It was true, the psychologist conceded during the first break, six hours in, that Baladin had talked about his disgust at the corruption present at every level of Russian government, that he had told detailed and undoubtedly true stories of huge sums stolen from state budgets to pay for ski chalets and private jets. He had described a friend dying in FSB custody following a power struggle for control of a municipal budget. He'd said with a shrug that his children were grown up and he was bored of his wife's greed and his mistress's immaturity. But he was emotionally flat when discussing these subjects, the psychologist insisted. His answers were inconsistent, unclear or simply too brief to be credible. It was impossible to see how they added up to the life-changing decision to defect.

Leonard went back in. He pressed harder. Baladin admitted having received and paid bribes himself. So what had changed to make him so outraged about the behaviour of others? Was it merely a question of scale? He was tired, Baladin said, as he floundered for an answer – it had now been eight hours since he'd started talking and he hadn't been allowed a proper break. Could he be permitted to stand in the fresh air and smoke a cigarette?

"Let me ask you a question first," said Leonard. "When your friend was killed by the FSB, did you help his widow? Given the circumstances of his death, she would have lost access to his pension, possibly also their apartment. She would have been in a very difficult position. Did you give her any money?"

"No," replied Baladin.

"But you visited her."

"No."

"You didn't even visit her?"

"No."

"Why not?"

He shrugged.

"How does it explain you coming to us?"

"I don't know. Maybe it doesn't."

"What are we doing here, Aleksandr?"

"I'm trying to give you what you want."

"I want to understand why you're here."

Baladin sighed. He was quiet for several minutes. "I've told you," he said.

"No, you haven't."

"I'm tired," he said. He crossed and uncrossed his legs.

"Why have you come to us?"

For a while Leonard thought the man had given up answering his questions.

"I visited your country when I was fifteen," Baladin said finally. "My father was a diplomat in The Hague. We took a train from London to Edinburgh, but there wasn't enough room for all of us in the carriage and because I was older than my brother and sister I was sent to sit on my own in the carriage next door. At first my father would check on me every half hour. But after a while he stopped coming. I had a small bag with a little bit of money, some English mints and a book of crossword puzzles to keep me busy. I still remember the stations. The names! Can you imagine my excitement at passing through Nottingham, or the way I stood on my toes for a glimpse of Sherwood Forest? A schoolgirl boarded the train in Doncaster. I watched her on the platform saying goodbye to her boyfriend, and although I had no experience of girls I could tell that she did not love him. She sat in the same carriage as me. She was maybe seventeen or eighteen – a little older. When the train conductor came she must have seen how nervous I was to use my English. Afterwards she stuck her tongue out at me and started asking questions. We talked for at least an hour. She was the prettiest girl I had ever talked to. Freckles on her nose, little blonde hairs on her knees. You have been to Russia, this much is clear. So you will know Russian girls don't smile at strangers on trains. We talked until Middlesbrough and then she got off the train and disappeared into the night. I looked for her on the platform to wave goodbye but I couldn't see her. It was only when my father came to collect me an hour later that I realized she had taken my bag." He looked at the wall. His eyes flickered as though watching a whole country flashing past at speed.

"Your very own Maid Marian," said Leonard.

Baladin rubbed his face and straightened up in the chair. "I missed an appointment to be here," he said. "If someone in my position misses an appointment in a European capital, people start worrying very quickly. But you want to be certain, so here we are, eight hours later."

"You must understand that it's essential —"

"You don't think I'm real, is that it?"

"It doesn't add up, Aleksandr. Your story, it just —"

"Enough," Baladin said. "I'm tired. I'm tired of you, whatever your name is. We have people like you in Moscow – maybe *that's* why I want to leave. Make your damn decision and let me go."

It wasn't Leonard's decision to make. He was asked to come down on one side or the other, of course, as were the two analysts and the psychologist, and he did just that. An hour later Baladin was dropped off on a quiet street around the corner from a train station. His Burberry scarf tugged this way and that in the breeze. No one was surprised when he boarded a flight to Moscow the next day. Everyone understood it as confirmation that he had been a dangle, as they'd suspected, and Leonard was widely praised for having used the sustained pressure of his character to expose the implausibilities in the man's story.

Over the coming weeks and months Leonard kept an unofficial eye on Baladin from afar. He watched him return to his job in the ministry, he watched him fail to be promoted, he watched him leave his wife, argue with his children, get into fights, drink too much. Soon afterwards Leonard moved teams and lost access to the reporting. He never found out what happened to Baladin. But he had already come to the conclusion that he had probably been sincere in his wish to defect. For a long time he didn't know what to make of that. Maybe the decision to change sides is such a momentous one that the motivation for it can be hard to explain. Maybe it's a hundred different things wrapped up in one package and you have to accept that when you open it up it'll look a mess. Maybe the other side simply needs something it recognizes – something it has seen countless times before. Or maybe Baladin was just tired. Maybe he just wanted a cigarette.

Leonard sits in Willa's living room and studies his long, pale, unlovely reflection in the window. He has had a good first day and should be satisfied. Instead he feels an unfamiliar disquiet. It comes down to this, that Leonard is nothing if not a fast ball. He hurls himself at targets. His chief weapons, with which he has been known to cause considerable damage, are speed, surprise, precision and momentum. But on this occasion, when it comes to the case before him, he feels something unexpected – he feels spin. He doesn't know whether it is caused by a dip in the ground or by Remnant's delivery, but it's unmistakably there, a drifting, sliding sensation that leaves him dizzy. He closes his eyes and lets his breathing settle, going through the day hour by hour, and to his surprise it doesn't take long before he finds what is bothering him, but in that moment his phone rings and Remnant tells him to be ready for an urgent meeting first thing.

FROM THE ARCHIVES

2A

Handbook of Operational Techniques
Chapter 42 Section vi

SUBJECT: Rapid Intelligence Generation (RIG)

164. Rapid Intelligence Generation (informally referred to
      by case officers as "Rigging" or "Shaking the Tree") is an
      operational technique used to identify new intelligence
      at speed in a context where none previously existed.

165. RIG is typically used in the aftermath of a serious incident.
      In such a scenario, if the investigative team is in urgent
      need of new leads, an officer may be deployed into a
      community, neighbourhood or other location under a
      light and flexible cover to harvest as much intelligence
      as possible in as short a time as possible.

166. RIG is a high-risk technique used sparingly and only
      when no alternative exists, as it runs contrary to our
      long-established principles governing covert action, spe-
      cifically the value we place on remaining undetected. The

officer will need to make every effort to conceal their role and the reason for their interest in the topic at hand. However, as the primary objective of a RIG deployment is to generate new intelligence in a short time frame, it must be accepted that the risk of exposure and compromise is unnaturally high. It is this *elevated risk* that distinguishes RIG from other operational techniques.

167. A backup team must be positioned in the vicinity in case urgent exfiltration is required.

Case Study

168. Following the suspicious death of a dissident on UK soil, an officer was deployed under light cover to visit London bars and cafes popular with the Russian émigré community. Given the extensive ties between many wealthy expatriates and the Russian state, the officer was tasked to collect as much ground-level speculation about the death as possible over the course of a single day.

169. The officer succeeded in eliciting the names of two Moscow-based individuals believed to have been involved in the planning of the murder, and the name of a third individual, a UK national, rumoured to have provided logistical support.

170. In the final phase of the deployment, the officer was accused by a Russian businessman of being an undercover journalist and forcefully ejected from the premises by security personnel, requiring hospital treatment.

2B

SUBJECT: Transcript: Death of Aleksandr BALADIN in custody

DATE: 29 May 2014

Boris OBLONSKY is summoned to the phone by his wife.

Andrei KUZNETSOV asks OBLONSKY if he has heard the news about Aleksandr [by context Aleksandr BALADIN].

KUZNETSOV says that Aleksandr was left in a cell overnight with a criminal and found dead the next morning by the guards. KUZNETSOV says that the cause of death was recorded as drowning, which nobody can understand. He speculates that this looks like something the FSB arranged.

OBLONSKY asks about the funeral. He says he does not understand what happened to Aleksandr or how it happened so quickly. He says one minute he is a respected official and the next minute he is drunk at a Victory Day party, trying to punch his boss. OBLONSKY says if his own father was an ex-ambassador with influence rather than a schoolteacher he would not throw it all away like Aleksandr.

KUZNETSOV reminds OBLONSKY of the time when they were students and their professor gave OBLONSKY such a low grade that he had to repeat the year. Even though Aleksandr received the best grade in the year, everyone suspected he was the one responsible for stealing the keys to the professor's car and packing every inch of the interior with snow, including the glove compartment and the boot. KUZNETSOV and OBLONSKY agree that it would be a mistake to attend Aleksandr's funeral but instead make plans to meet for a quiet drink to raise a glass to their friend.

TOP SECRET

2C

SUBJECT: Behavioural Science Unit analysis

DATE: 24 May 2019

1. On 17 May, the Behavioural Science Unit (BSU) was asked by Gatekeeping to carry out an assessment of a retirement card intended for a Subject of Interest (SOI) suspected of working as an agent for the Russian state. (We understand that the SOI left the Service at short notice and did not return to collect the card.) In particular, we were asked whether the comments written in the card reveal anything about the SOI's character and reputation that might be relevant to the Gatekeeping investigation.

2. For reasons of confidentiality, all names were redacted by Gatekeeping before the card was passed to the BSU.

3. We have omitted the majority of the comments in the card from our analysis below as in our judgement they do not reveal anything of interest. The comments below are what is left; they are grouped according to theme.

Analysis

a)   Dear ▮▮, I couldn't believe it when I heard you were
     leaving! This makes me the old-timer in the team now...
     [drawing of sad face] Don't be a stranger! Love, ▮▮▮▮

*BSU comment: It may be that the SOI's former status as the oldest
member of the team reflected a failure to progress up the ranks in the
normal manner. For an individual with an overdeveloped sense of
grievance, this could act as a trigger for betrayal. A recent example of
this is the case of Edward Devenney, a Royal Navy submariner who
was convicted of attempting to pass classified material to the Russians
after being passed over for promotion.*

b)   At last your rid of us! Enjoy a happy retirement! ▮▮▮ PS.
     Can you fill up the photocopier before you go?
c)   What, no leaving drinks?! There's a surprise ... NOT! Best
     wishes for your retirement!! ▮▮▮▮

*BSU comment: The tone of b) and c) is slightly more aggressive than
we would expect from a retirement card. These comments suggest the
SOI was perceived as aloof and not a "team player", and may mean the
SOI was subject to criticism from some quarters. Peer-to-peer criticism
in the workplace often takes the form of "banter" of a kind that can
easily cross over into unpleasantness. If this is what happened in this
case, it might have contributed to the SOI's feeling of marginalization
and acted as a trigger for betrayal.*

d)   Dear ▮▮, I wish I'd had the chance to get to know you
     better! For a new joiner like me you've really embodied the

quiet reliability that is the hallmark of this office. Thank you for all your kindness! I'll miss you! ▮

BSU comment: We note the discrepancy here. b) and c) suggest the SOI was aloof whereas d) comments on their "kindness". We have observed in previous cases that double agents can be highly charming but select with great care the people to whom they display their charm. To all others they are content to appear remote and uninteresting. It may therefore be that the SOI was "grooming" the author of d) for an unknown purpose and that d) merits further investigation by Gatekeeping.

e) Happy retirement! Enjoy ruling the world from your secret volcano HQ! ▮

f) We've had a pool on why you're leaving a year early – my money says that Cyclops in Gatekeeping has finally caught up with you! Off to the Tower! No wonder, you've let in some right odd fish over the years… xxx ▮

BSU comment: People often make a judgement about someone without having firm evidence to justify it. Studies have shown that this "thin-slicing" can be very accurate. In our experience, a double agent's colleagues are often aware that something is wrong but lack the evidence to back up their suspicions and so never report it. e) and f) appear to suggest colleagues intuited that the SOI was engaged in harmful activities.

g) Dear ▮, On behalf of the entire management team, I'd like to thank you for your many years of quiet and steadfast industry. We wish you the best for your retirement. We will all miss your quiet, agreeable presence in the team. ▮

BSU comment: Although this is a bland managerial comment of the sort that might appear in any retirement card, we note its muted tone, as well as the fact that no other senior managers added a comment, despite the SOI being a long-serving member of staff. This might suggest that the SOI kept a deliberately low profile. In that context, the repetition of "quiet" is interesting. Philby was noted by his Russian handler to be "timid and irresolute", qualities that meant he could be easily manipulated. We wonder whether this SOI, with their "agreeable" nature, possesses similar characteristics.

TOP SECRET

CHAPTER THREE

"We've made a discovery," says Charles Remnant.

It is clear from a small tilt of his head that the credit belongs to Franny, the young woman next to him. They are sitting in a cramped attic flat a few streets from Regent's Park that Leonard has been allocated for the duration of the investigation. It was bought in 1960 to facilitate a surveillance operation against a resident on the third floor, and although it's permanently on the verge of being sold, something has always come along to justify its retention: a trade union leader who entertained his mistress two floors down, a Pakistani nuclear scientist across the road, a temporary consulate around the corner. In quieter times it's loaned to staff with an operational requirement to be central. It comes equipped with a secure line to the office and a safe containing cash, unregistered mobile phones, a camera, eavesdropping kit and other items Leonard might need.

"Our discovery changes things quite significantly," says Remnant.

For something intended for use in covert operations, the flat looks remarkably like government property: the furniture is cheap and old, the carpet threadbare, and

73

every room smells of stale cigarette smoke. It's hard to imagine anyone who could afford this neighbourhood living in such conditions. A pair of French windows opens onto a small balcony, and even at this early hour – they rang his doorbell at eight o'clock – the heat is smotheringly fierce. Remnant is dressed in a tweed blazer and striped tie. He is sweating profusely from the climb. He dabs his forehead with a folded handkerchief like a nurse dabbing the forehead of a fever-ridden patient they wish would hurry up and die.

"We don't normally introduce Gatekeepers to each other unless there's a compelling reason," Remnant continues. "In this case, there are two. The first is that the deadline for your investigation into Willa Karlsson has been brought forward by one week to this Friday. So you may need some help."

The sleeves of Leonard's white shirt are buttoned at the wrist despite the heat. He is thinking about the difference between London rooftops and London streets.

"You look distracted," says Remnant.

The rooftops in this very exclusive neighbourhood appear to have remained unchanged for generations, as though with each stair you climbed another year into the past. The spires, domes, chimney pots and garret windows bring to his mind Mary Poppins and Peter Pan, daring escapes by men in black suits and bowler hats, a single bullet fired harmlessly over the head of a plucky pursuer. There's even a limp Union Jack waiting for the wind to pick up. Remnant belongs to rooftop London, Leonard thinks – with his tweed, with his glass eye.

"Are you listening?" says Remnant.

Five floors below them London streets elbow and jostle and fizz in ten million different directions. London streets don't let up. He's only just met her, but Franny looks as though she belongs to *that* London, Leonard thinks. "Instead of having ten days to find out if Willa is a Russian spy," he says, "I've now got five."

"In total, yes," says Remnant. "Four days from now. I know it's tight, but we're hopeful you still might turn up something of value."

"Why, out of interest?" asks Leonard.

Remnant looks at Franny.

"I've been taking a passive look at the data," she says.

It's hard to imagine her doing anything passively. She is wearing oxblood Doc Marten boots and a military-green jumpsuit that is elasticated at the waist. Curly ink-black hair is gathered loosely at her neck. Remnant isn't a particularly short man and she is taller than him by several inches.

"As you know, I can't request new data as that would leave a footprint," she says, "and we're trying to run this investigation discreetly. But I've found a Russian national who flew into Heathrow ten days before Willa was poisoned and then left two days later. The passport number's suspiciously close to one used by the Russians for a technical operation in The Hague six months ago."

"This increases the likelihood of Russian involvement," says Remnant. "As a result we'll need to inform the Home Secretary earlier than planned. It's important you understand the impact on risk too. This is the other reason for bringing in Franny. We want another officer to know where you are at all times, given that there may well be someone else – someone with hostile intentions – operating in the same space as you." Remnant refolds his handkerchief and scrapes his forehead with the stiff edge. "What do you think, Leonard?"

"I think we'd better get a move on." Leonard points at the laptop by Franny's feet. "Does that thing work?"

She nods.

"I assume you've got access to Willa's records," he says. "How much personal leave did she take in her last year?"

Franny's shoulders are as broad and strong as a swimmer's. She opens the laptop and applies herself to the matter of passwords and decryption. Remnant steps through the French windows onto the tiny square balcony. He is framed against the blue sky like a high diver at the end of the board.

She has found what she was looking for. "Willa took leave in small increments – a few days here and there," she says. "In total she requested eight blocks over the last year, ranging from a single day to a full week."

"There's a landline in her flat," says Leonard. "Are there any gaps in her use of it that overlap with her leave? In other words, times she may have been out of London?"

"She didn't use her landline much. I've been looking at what little there is for a few weeks now." She taps a button. "Here it is. She made or answered phone calls during two of her leave periods – one outgoing to her doctor, lasting a little over two minutes, the other incoming from a distant cousin in Italy. But it'd be a mistake to place too much weight on that. During the six other periods of leave she might have been in London but simply out of the flat when someone called."

"You're right," says Leonard. "Take it as read that if we had time we'd test every assumption a dozen different ways. But what you're telling me is that there are two periods of leave when Willa *probably* didn't leave London and six periods of leave when she *might* have done. Within those six we're looking for something that feels like a regular appointment. Even Russian agent handlers operating behind enemy lines need an element of predictability in their lives. More so if we're looking at a sustained relationship over a long period of time."

Remnant comes in from the balcony. "Predictability? Wouldn't her handler have tried to make it look random?"

"In theory, yes. In practice it's quite hard to do. You don't want to meet your agent too often because there are risks attached to each meeting, and in many cases it's not an enjoyable encounter – especially if the agent is unhappy or demanding. But you also don't want to leave it too long between meetings because you're keen to get the intelligence, deliver new tasking and deal with any new problems. So in every relationship between a handler and their agent there's a sweet spot – a perfectly sized gap. It might be a week or a month or a year, it depends on the circumstances. But a pattern will usually emerge. Do you remember that Georgian military attaché we kicked out a couple of years ago? He had to pick up his daughter from ballet at five and his wife would lose her temper if he was late for their bridge group at eight, so he always had to squeeze his operational work into that window. We were able to set our watches by him, he was so punctual. Life goes on, even for spies."

Franny continues to tap at the keyboard.

"You're assuming Willa had to request leave in order to attend meetings with her handler," says Remnant. "Isn't it possible she met him in London – in her local pub, for example?"

"He's probably an illegal, posted here under deep cover on a long-term basis. Willa never went abroad, and there's no way the Russians would have flown an officer in every few months to see her. That's far too risky. So the question is, where would an illegal base himself? I think he'd choose somewhere remote. He'd sit tight and make Willa take all the risks by travelling to see him – that's how the Russians work. They protect themselves."

Franny looks up. "It's not much of a pattern, but three of the six leave periods occur next to weekends," she says. "There's a Thursday, Friday and Monday in September, the same in January, and then a Monday to Wednesday in April. The other three are midweek. A couple of Tuesdays and a Tuesday–Wednesday."

Leonard leans forward in his chair. "That gives us trips out of London every three to four months, which is a kind of pattern," he says. "According to her hairdresser, Willa complained about young men on trains not giving up their seats, so let's assume she took the train. I found two Oyster cards in her flat. The machines at stations allow you to see the last eight journeys." He takes out a slim notebook. "April, you said. That'll be the most recent one. We're in luck. On Saturday, 7 April she took the Tube to Liverpool Street, arriving at 10.37. And then on Sunday, the twenty-ninth, using the other card, she went to Euston, arriving at 14.35."

"It's the first of those," says Franny. "She took the ninth, tenth and eleventh as annual leave. So you're saying that on 7 April she travelled from Liverpool Street to somewhere outside London and that based on your idea about routine and patterns this trip may have been significant. But where did she go?"

"This is one of the books I found in Willa's flat," Leonard says, reaching for his bag. "*Birds of the British Isles: A Field Guide.* She doesn't have many books, but this one looks well used. There are a dozen or so pages in particular that look slightly more worn than the others."

"How's that of any use?" says Remnant.

"The question Leonard's asking," says Franny, picking up the book, "is whether any of the birds on those dozen or so pages are found in areas you might travel to from Liverpool Street. Isn't that right?" She begins to turn the pages carefully. "This looks like rain damage, it's got that stiff, crinkled feel to it. And this page has been folded at the corner. Let's start here. 'The pink-footed goose can be observed near the Ribble, the Solway, the Wash and along the east Scottish coast'," she reads. "Someone keep track of this." She turns more pages. "This one's only found in Wales, we can rule it out. Something's been spilled here – tea or coffee, I think. 'The hawfinch is found in the Forest of Dean, the New Forest, the East Anglian Breckland and North Wales.' There's a Norfolk theme developing. Here's another one. 'Sightings of the little tern are frequently recorded in Great Yarmouth, Norfolk, Minsmere, Suffolk and Hampshire.'"

"There was a block of Norfolk fudge in her cupboards," says Leonard.

"Trains from Liverpool Street go to Norfolk," says Remnant.

"I've got the timetable from that week," says Leonard. "Willa arrived at Liverpool Street at 10.37. The next fast train to Norwich is at 11.31 – that's almost an hour's wait. But there's a slower train with more stops at 10.52. That time works better."

Franny looks up at the ceiling to think. "So let's say she was going to Norfolk but not to Norwich. Let's say she was going to one of the smaller stations on the way. Which ones are only serviced by the slower train?"

"Colchester, Manningtree, Stowmarket and Diss."

"Diss is the only one of those in Norfolk," says Remnant. "That gets us somewhere. But it's still a lot of ground to cover in four days. Franny, is there anything in her phone records that connects her to Norfolk?"

"Give me a few minutes."

"Let's have a look on the way," says Leonard. "There's a train in just over thirty minutes that we can catch if we hurry."

"We?" says Remnant. "I can't possibly just —"

"Not you, Charles," says Franny, standing up. At full height she has to stoop slightly beneath the sloped ceiling. She smiles for the first time. "Leave the hunt for the pink-footed goose to us."

Tuesday, 0929

LIVERPOOL STREET TO COLCHESTER

They board seconds before the train pulls out of the station. The air conditioning isn't working. Franny tries to slide open a window but it won't budge – Leonard isn't sure it's meant to open at all. But before he can say anything she rolls up the sleeves of her green jumpsuit and shifts her feet and adjusts her grip on the lip of the window and pulls it open with such explosive force that the metal frame bends away from the carriage. Everyone turns around to see what has happened. Oblivious to the stares, she bends over to unzip the laptop case.

"So you think there's something Norfolk-related on there, do you?" Leonard says, raising his voice to be heard over the noise of the wind rushing in through the open window.

"I'm pretty sure I've seen something," she says, sitting down opposite him. "I've got her personnel records, bank statements, work history and plenty besides that. She may well have gone to Norfolk to conduct a vetting interview at some point. I've also got more than twenty years of landline billing. It's hard to avoid leaving any trace, even for a person like Willa who flies under the radar."

"She must be the worst possible target for you."

"How so?"

Franny has cut herself in the process of opening the window. Leonard passes her his handkerchief. She wipes her finger clean before starting to type.

"She's hard to see in data," says Leonard.

"Some people leave very clear imprints, others very faint ones. But they're usually there if you know where to look. Even the absence of data can be telling. Take mobiles, for example. People think that turning a phone off makes them disappear. Which it does, in some ways. But it also highlights that they're doing something they want to conceal."

"I'm not sure how that'll help us with Willa," he says. "She didn't even have a phone."

Franny squints at him, unsure whether he's needling her or has misunderstood the point she was making. "I know that better than anyone," she says, turning back to the laptop. "I'm making a general point about the imprint left in data."

"All this talk of imprints. It sounds as though you're examining a shroud."

This time she ignores him.

"I wonder if it's a kind of faith," he says, "this idea that technology can answer every question."

She leans in to look at the screen more closely.

"Data as the new religion," he says, getting nowhere. He looks out of the window. "You're its high priestess, the laptop your silver chalice. You're preparing to mediate —"

"Or I could just have a look and see what's there," she says, her voice rising slightly despite her best efforts. "That'll tell us whether data can answer the question in this particular instance, which is all that really matters." And then, in case she's been too direct: "Not that your wider philosophical point isn't an interesting one, Leonard."

"I have no reason to doubt the answer is somewhere on your laptop. It's your confidence that puzzles me."

"If you agree the answer is probably there, isn't my confidence well placed?" she asks.

"It seems instinctive. It's a reflex action."

The train picks up speed and the wind rushing into the carriage makes conversation difficult. As Franny rises to her feet, more than a few of their fellow passengers turn to watch her, curious to see what she'll do this time. They look almost disappointed when she simply bends the metal frame back into shape and slides the window shut.

"What?" she says.

"I was just saying that your confidence in data seems a reflex action."

She sighs. "We've only just met, Leonard. Isn't it a little early to decide what my reflex actions are?"

"Do you play poker? Often the best time to get the measure of your opponent is when they first sit down, before they get a chance to settle into the game, find their rhythm, that sort of thing."

"Your *opponent*?"

"I don't mean you're —"

"Yes, you do."

"No —"

"You know, Leonard, they use some of your operations as case studies in training. I don't know how many of your interviews we listened to in total, but it was enough to identify the techniques you use to unsettle your interviewees before they even sit down. It's about which chair you give them, and limiting their personal space, and being overly personal and then suddenly formal. Is that right? I have to say, I didn't think I'd get the chance to be on the receiving end of it so soon."

"That's not —"

"I'm really, really looking forward to working with you. You have a reputation for getting things done. You also have a reputation for talking to every single person as though you're interrogating them. As though everyone's got a secret and it's your job to find it out. So shall we get your questions out of the way? That'll save you the bother of provoking me into disclosures. What do you want to know?"

"No, I —"

"I'll tell you what *everyone* wants to know, let's start there. My name is actually Saffron, which comes from the Persian word zafran, but everyone calls me Franny, even my – what was your word? – my *opponents*. My grandmother was Iranian. I'm five foot eleven, I wrestle for fun, I know more than a few ways to snap your arm off. The weather up here is the same as the weather everywhere else. Tell me when to stop. I like science fiction, swimming in rivers, art galleries, Simon and Garfunkel, going on holiday by myself. Anything else? I have —"

She is interrupted by the siren of a small child's scream. An unopened can of Fanta rolls down the aisle towards them. In one single fluid motion Franny extends an oxblood boot and kicks the can back where it came from so hard that it leaves the floor and crashes into something at the other end. The screaming stops.

"Tell me something," she says, turning to Leonard. "What did you learn about Willa from walking around her neighbourhood yesterday?"

"Not a huge amount. That she sometimes went away by train, that she was friends of a kind with her local priest, that she might have been able to read Russian."

"Imagine the world twenty years from now," she says. "Let's assume it's cashless and that facial recognition technology is pretty good. Is there anything you found yesterday that couldn't also be found in data?"

"It's hard to argue against a set of imaginary future capabilities such —"

"Wait, you think facial recognition is imaginary?"

"No —"

"There's nothing imaginary about it," she says.

"Still —"

"Try your best."

"We'd know where Willa went, you're right," he says. "We'd know what books she bought. But there are other things."

"Like what? Give me an insight."

"Let me see. The paint in her flat is expensive but her handbag is cheap."

"Of all the examples…" Franny looks surprised and amused in equal measure. "If you applied the right algorithm to her spending history it'd spot an anomaly like that straight away. It's just numbers – it's just more data. A program could work out an average price and identify inconsistencies in purchasing patterns in a fraction of a second." She shakes her head. "But for some reason you attach a magical quality to your observation, as though … as though each person walks around emitting unique odours and then you come along like a hound dog sniffing the air to intuit the core of their identity. It's a very old-fashioned idea. You say I've got faith in data. But you've got faith in character. That's much more irrational."

"You're completely right," Leonard says, smiling. It surprises him how much he is enjoying talking to Franny. "It was a poor example. All I'm saying is that character isn't reducible to a data set. There's something else, some other quality —"

"Here we go."

"What do you mean?"

"No, please – go on."

"No, tell me."

"You're going to say it."

"Say what?"

"The word, Leonard. You're going to say the word."

"What word?"

She closes her eyes. "Soul," she whispers.

He laughs. "Well, why not? It's as good a word as any, Franny. I'm not saying intuition is superior to data. I can see that in some ways it's just another data point, and often an imperfect one, once you've factored in bias, prejudice, ignorance and so on. But it does seem to me that a kind of creative intuition can access areas a computer program can't. I suppose it is a belief, you're right. But intuition is subtle, it's flexible. It's a two-way process. An intuition tells me something about the other person and about myself. It's a creative act that's different for each person who engages in it."

It's her turn to laugh. "You're so out of touch, Leonard. I mean, a decade at least. You've got no idea what's around the corner. What you said, that's the definition of artificial intelligence. It *learns*, you know. It changes, it grows, it adapts. It's not just an Excel spreadsheet on a larger scale. Your example of the handbag and the paint would be spotted in a heartbeat. Can you really not do any better than that?"

He looks out of the window but his eyes catch on pulsing reflections of the carriage interior – on a rip in the seat, an orange plastic bag, the liquid quality of sunlight, as though Franny's black hair has been dipped in gold. However hard he tries, he can't break through to the world out there. You think you're looking out, but the truth is that you're always looking in.

"It seems like we've reversed roles," says Franny. "Now I'm the one giving you a hard time."

"You went to all that trouble to open the window," says Leonard, "breaking it in the process and alarming the other passengers. But then you thought nothing of closing it a few minutes later when the situation changed."

A warm blush wraps itself around Franny's neck. "I'm asking about Willa, not me." She sounds angry. "Anyway, so what?"

"I don't know. It tells me something. It tells me you're unusual."

"*That's* your insight?"

"Yes."

"Wow." She turns back to the laptop. "*I'm* unusual," she says quietly, as though to herself. She presses a key. "The rat-catcher thinks *I'm* unusual."

"I intended the word as a —"

"Hang on," she says. "Look here. A call from Willa's landline nine years ago to what looks like a country hotel in Norfolk. Twenty minutes by car from Diss. Do you want to call them or shall I?"

COLCHESTER TO MANNINGTREE

The doors open. Teenage boys on a school trip pour into the carriage like a lurid energy drink. By the time the train pulls out of the station most of the other passengers have moved elsewhere. Leonard takes stock of their uniforms. They clearly think wearing them like this – shirts untucked, buttons undone, ties descending to mid-chest – makes a mockery of the idea of a uniform. *You think you can control us. You can't control us.* But of course they all wear their uniforms in exactly the same incorrect way. It reminds him how much he hates groups of any kind.

Franny hangs up. "We've got a garden room for two nights," she says. "What's our cover? Are you still going to say you're Willa's long-lost nephew?"

He shakes his head. "Anyone who knows her at all will know she doesn't have a nephew. Let's keep it simple. We're neighbours of hers in London and she recommended the place for a getaway."

One of the schoolboys – short, skinny, his voice unbroken – has wandered down to have a look at them. "Are you two fucking?" he asks loudly.

The teacher looks up from his phone. "Shut up, Daniels."

"She'd break him in half, sir."

The boys' hysterical laughter is pegged not to the quality of the joke but to the scale of the offence.

"Daniels, I won't tell you again. Back to your seat."

"Sorry, sir." The boy saunters back to his friends, stopping on the way to examine the contents of a bin. He's just keeping his head above water, thinks Leonard.

"I haven't had any operational training," says Franny. "I've been desk-based since I joined. So when we get to the hotel I'll follow your lead."

"I suspect you'll be a natural. You've got a very likeable manner."

"There's no need to be sarcastic, Leonard."

"What? No, no, I —"

"Don't worry, you don't have to —"

89

"No, I … there's one thing to say before we get there. Remnant might have told you this already, but our objective is to get answers, not play it safe. It can take a bit of getting used to, given how careful we normally are as an office. We'll stick to our story and try to be discreet. But if some of our questions need to go a bit close to the bone to get where we want, that's fine."

"Understood."

"It can be fun," he says. "Stick out your elbows and knock over some china."

"Didn't you get beaten up doing something like this once?"

"A couple of slaps from a security guard who got carried away."

"I thought it was more than that."

"Maybe a little bit more. I asked one question too many and his boss decided I was a journalist. He'd been on the receiving end of some bad press and took the opportunity to deliver his feedback directly to me. More satisfying than writing a letter to the editor, I imagine."

The train creeps behind garden fences like a burglar looking for an open window.

"Sir, can I put my sunglasses on?" It's the same boy. "I know it's not normally allowed but —"

"What are you talking about now, Daniels?"

"I'm getting a shine off that guy's bald head. Right into my eyes. It's a real risk, sir. If he cocked his head at the wrong angle he could blind a pilot and bring down a plane full of people."

"I won't tell you again, Daniels."

"Sorry, sir."

Even though the material is banal, Leonard admires the skill of the boy's delivery, his insouciance, the mastery he displays over his teacher. Each exchange of *I won't tell you again* and *sorry, sir* is so patently untrue on both sides that it merely underscores Daniels's triumph. It is as though they are re-enacting a battle won long ago for the entertainment – and education – of the other boys.

"What are we trying to find out?" asks Franny. "Beyond the obvious."

"If Willa ever stayed in the hotel, how many times, whether they saw her with someone else. We're trying to find a thread we can follow on to the next place."

"You mentioned that her handler – let's assume she had one – would probably have been a Russian illegal. What does that mean in terms of his profile?"

"It's hard to say," says Leonard. "He would have stolen someone else's identity – typically the identity of a baby that died – and made it look as real as possible over the years by acquiring other documentation. There was a network of illegals brought down in the US a few years ago. Some of them claimed to be Canadian, others said they were from South America."

"And he'll have fled, won't he? After Willa was poisoned?"

"Probably. It'd be very risky for him to stay in the country. But it's possible he's running other agents and hasn't yet been able to hand them over to someone else, or he thinks he's got away with it, or that —"

"Is that called a jumpsuit, sir?" the boy calls out.

"What's that, Daniels?"

"Is that what they wear for parachute jumps, sir?"

"Daniels, sit down and leave the people alone."

"It's a serious question, sir. Don't you teach science? It's just, you know, the laws of gravity and that. I would have thought there's a limit to the weight a parachute's able to support, that's all. I mean, if you pushed an elephant out of a plane, sir, let's say she's wearing a jumpsuit, to make it realistic —"

"I won't tell you again, Daniels."

"Sorry, sir."

Leonard starts to turn around. Franny puts out a hand to stop him.

"It's like being back at school," he says.

"You too? It wasn't my favourite time either. But I've worked out a coping strategy. One that helps me stay centred and balanced."

Franny stands up. The boys all turn to look at her. Even the teacher looks up from his phone.

"Let's see what you can deduce about my character from this," she whispers down to Leonard.

She draws herself up to her full height.

"Daniels?" she sings out. "You're a prick."

The carriage goes quiet.

MANNINGTREE TO STOWMARKET

When Leonard used to think about growing up, about the bullying and the violence and the unhappiness, there were several things he struggled to understand. Chief among them was how something could feel impossibly distant in one moment and incredibly vivid in the next. It made no sense that something he hadn't been consciously aware of for years retained the power to overwhelm him. Why did the potency of so much fail to diminish with time? How did he stand in relation to his own past? The explanation he has arrived at in adulthood – the only explanation that makes any sense to him – is that time is not laid out like a running track, with birth as the starting line and chalk markings every ten metres to indicate how far he has travelled. Instead he believes there is no such thing as distance. He believes everything is happening all the time. In the same way a reader accesses a book page by page, and in a certain order, Leonard accepts he has no choice but to access his life one page at a time, as we all do. But he believes the other pages continue to exist in the same moment. It is meaningless to say they have gone, that they are no longer here. They *are* here, they are happening *now*. There is no other explanation for the way he experiences life. And this is why he chooses to be how he is, whatever other people might think of him, because he has to be strong for the ten-year-old Leonard who at this moment is being dragged into a storeroom by a group of older boys for a beating that will leave him with a limp for at least a month, the ten-year-old

Leonard who will only go on to survive his childhood because of the strength he draws from another version of himself, a version he's not even aware of yet, a version whose response to a beating from a Russian bodyguard is not to curl up and protect himself but to kick out so hard his assailant's knee crumples the wrong way. He is able to endure the mockery of his teachers because he refuses to be intimidated by Remnant. He is able to cope with the disappearance of his father because there is no one in his adult life he can't afford to lose. He is able to survive the jokes, the loneliness, the lesson that he isn't good enough for one reason and one reason only, and that's because right now Leonard does not back down for anyone, at any time, under any circumstances.

He knows this would sound crazy. He's relieved he'll never have to put it into words.

STOWMARKET TO DISS

"This thing about sharing a room," says Franny.

"I don't want to make you feel uncomfortable. I'll sleep on the floor, of course. Or in the bathroom. It's just that it looks odd for two single people of the opposite sex to go away together. It looks like they're colleagues, and then people start to wonder what their job is. Far better to stay away from all that and use a cover story that fits into an easily recognizable category."

"So we're a couple."

"Don't worry," he says. "I won't touch you in public."

She pulls a face.

"Or in private," Leonard says quickly. "I don't mean —"

"I'm teasing you."

"Some of the old-school instructors insist you have to practise holding hands and the like because a couple who never touch look odd. But the truth is that most couples never touch."

"Do you never touch your girlfriend?" she asks.

"I don't have a girlfriend."

"Your boyfriend, then?"

"You're wasted as an analyst," he says. "You should be out in the field asking targets the hard questions."

"No, you're wasted in the *field*. The quickest way to get answers is not by interrogating targets, it's by interrogating their data."

"Let's imagine all you've got is the person sitting opposite you. What question would you ask to find out the answer?"

"I'd ask, can I borrow your phone to make a quick call? Once I've got it in my hands it would take about thirty seconds to find out the answer from your browsing history."

"What about your boyfriend?" Leonard asks.

Franny turns to the window. He watches the edges of her face – the dark downy hair at her temples, the sweat glistening around the base of her neck. "I don't have a boyfriend," she says finally. "My last boyfriend, though, I think he grew tired of touching me. At least that's how it felt."

"I'm sorry."

"There's something about a touch that's withdrawn that's worse than anything," she says. "It changes everything that came before it. Nothing was what you thought it was. It's not like one thing happened and was fine and then the next thing happened and wasn't fine, and the two things don't change each other. The present changes the past, the past changes the present. It's all so much more unstable than we think."

"I don't know how people cope."

"How do you cope, Leonard?"

"Did you ever read that fairy tale about the three brothers? They all wanted to impress their father, and so the first one became a blacksmith, the second one became a barber and the third a fencing master. When the time came to show off their skills, the blacksmith put four new shoes on a galloping horse and the barber shaved a hare in the field. But then it started to rain, and the third brother pulled out his sword and flourished it above his head with such speed and skill that not a drop of rain fell on him, even when the heavens opened."

"Mmm. Is that it?"

"Is that what?"

"Your answer."

"Too enigmatic?"

"A bit, yeah."

"I'm not sure what I mean," he says. "Never stop moving? Don't let anything get too close?"

"Even the rain. Was it hard to impress your father?"

"I wasn't able to stop him leaving, so I suppose the answer is yes."

"How old were you?"

"Ten."

"Did you try waving a stick around above your head to keep the rain off?"

"All the time." Leonard smiles. "At one point I carried a wooden sword with me everywhere. Other kids thought I was mad. Called me all sorts of things."

"Including rat-catcher?"

"Maybe not that one."

"I'm sorry," says Franny. "That was thoughtless."

"I don't mind it. It's just not meant as a term of affection, is it? It's still just other kids thinking I'm weird."

"I'll steer clear of it from now on. What *are* we going to call each other though? Darling? Sweetheart? You've got quite a forbidding manner, Leonard. If we're not going to touch each other at all, we've got to do something to make sure we look like a couple."

"That thing you said about me interrogating everyone. There'll be plenty of that with the people we come across in the next couple of days. There's not much I can do about that. It's what we're there for, after all. But I'll try to avoid doing it to you."

"That's how we'll look like a couple, is it, by you not interrogating me?"

"I am capable of acting naturally with a girl, Franny. At least I hope so. I have had girlfriends."

"Why do you do it?"

"Interrogate everyone? It's just my style, I suppose," says Leonard. "I can't be doing with any flimflam. But I have no problem if it comes back at me twice as hard."

"It's certainly a change from people who are nothing but flimflam."

"Some of our colleagues, you mean? I don't know, flimflam done well is a thing of beauty. It's just not my thing. I suspect the job doesn't help. I spend most of my days trying to pin bad people into a corner. It brings out certain qualities. Sometimes I get the sense that management would like to keep me in the basement and wheel me out for the awkward jobs."

"It doesn't sound as though you love the place," she says.

"I don't love organizations or institutions, that's the conclusion I've come to. But I love the work. That's enough to keep me there. Especially when they let me out to play on my own."

"Ouch."

"I'm very happy you're here, Franny. I just mean that's my temperament, to work on my own. I'm giving you fair warning, in case you find me difficult."

The loudspeaker announces that they'll arrive at their station in five minutes.

"That went quickly," Franny says. She switches off the laptop and packs it away. "I'm not sure we've completely sorted out our cover story, sweetheart."

Leonard knows from professional experience that a compliment is always a compliment, even when the other party suspects it might be insincere, and from personal experience that an insult offered in jest still leaves a mark. But he is surprised to find that an endearment offered in the same spirit remains an endearment, and for a brief moment he has to take himself in hand.

"Leonard?" says Franny.

"After this train journey, I wonder whether we should go for the bickering couple look."

"This holiday is a last-ditch attempt to reconnect and save our relationship."

"Which will only work if you're a bit less argumentative than usual," he says.

"Steady on."

"Just getting into character. Your turn."

"There you go again, telling me what to do," she says.

"Someone's got to."

"You're not my boss."

"It certainly feels like work," he says, "spending time with you."

An elderly couple turn to look at them. Leonard stands up to take his bag from the luggage rack.

"What *is* your job, by the way?" she asks. "I should probably know that. I've always thought the corduroy ensemble makes you look a bit like an expert on the *Antiques Roadshow*. One of the slightly less cool ones. Either that or the farmer in that famous painting. What's it called?"

"*American Gothic*. Let's say … I'm an art historian."

They are both standing now. The swaying of the train as it slows momentarily knocks them together. Leonard has to put a hand on Franny's arm to stop himself falling completely.

"Get off me," she says.

"Sorry."

"My dad warned me you were a pig," Franny says.

"Charles? What does he know —"

"Wait, *Charles?*" she says too loudly. They are carrying their bags down the aisle towards the doors. She stops abruptly and turns to face him. "Charles Remnant is my *dad* in this story?"

"You two are peas in a —"

"Fuck off, Leonard. That's taking things too far."

The train comes to a stop alongside the platform.

"That sort of language isn't going to help," Leonard says, catching the eye of the elderly couple and shaking his head disapprovingly. "Let's try to have a nice couple of days, see if we can rekindle that spark."

Franny is first through the doors and doesn't wait for him. "You certainly know how to sweep a girl off her feet," he hears her say as she strides off down the platform.

Tuesday, 1325

THE RECEPTIONIST

"What a lovely hotel you have here," says Leonard. "We heard it was special, didn't we, darling? But we didn't expect anything quite so charming as this."

Wooden beams cross the low, tilted ceiling at different angles. The light is dim and watery; Leonard has the sensation of being inside a sinking galleon slowly breaking apart beneath the waves. Franny nods enthusiastically as she turns to take it all in, the ploughshare and wheat sheaves and brown furniture turned black with dirt, but not before a look of distaste darts beneath the smiling surface of her face. "How many bedrooms do you have?" she asks.

"Twenty-one." The receptionist is friendly enough considering that at no point during their conversation has she stopped playing solitaire on the computer. "You're lucky we're so quiet at the moment, especially with this glorious weather." A tube of cigarette ash on the windowsill next to her rolls from side to side in the breeze. She waves a hand to get rid of the lingering smell. "I've put you in seventeen, it's got a lovely view of the pond."

"I'm looking forward to being woken up by birdsong rather than traffic," says Franny. "Has the hotel been here a long time?"

"As a hotel?" The receptionist looks up. "Oh, thirty years or more. It started off with just this building, and over the years the owners have added bits and pieces." She reaches under the desk to switch on a fan. "The house itself was built in 1634."

"One of our neighbours in London recommended you," says Leonard. "Willa Karlsson, do you know —"

"Oh, Willa – yes!" She smiles and sits upright. He thinks of the TV set his mother owned and the way it would snap from black-and-white to colour when you gave it a gentle knock on the side. "She's been coming here for so long, she's part of the furniture. I think she's due next week, isn't that right? Or is it the week after? I should really know. She's so regular – she makes her next booking as she's checking out."

"It's such a shame we couldn't overlap," he says. "How long is it she's been coming?"

"Longer than I've been working here, so at least eight or nine years. She's the only guest guaranteed to get a room whenever she wants. Always room nine, too. You know, for obvious reasons. We can't put someone like her upstairs, can we?"

"Of *course* you can't," says Leonard, as though the idea is unthinkable.

Franny finishes her examination of a portrait and turns back to the receptionist. "Such a shame for Willa, though, isn't it?" she says. "I bet the views are better on the top floor. Is there no way she can get up there?"

"Well, we haven't got a stairlift, if that's what you mean. They came in a few years ago to look at installing one but the corridors in a house this old are just too narrow."

"I can see that," says Leonard. "And I suppose it'd be too much…" He makes a large elaborate sweeping gesture with both hands that might mean anything at all.

"Exactly," she says. "It'd be a bit much for her to go up and down all day, wouldn't it? I suspect that stick of hers would take more than a bit of paint off the walls in the process." She swivels around to a board where the room keys are hung in neat rows. Leonard peers over her shoulder. At a quick glance it looks as though number nine is unoccupied. "I'm surprised she told you about us," the receptionist says, laying a set of keys on the counter. "She always says we're her best-kept secret."

"Oh, believe me, she made us promise a hundred times not to tell anyone," Leonard says. "But I can't believe she's been coming here for close to ten years and we're the first people she's told. Has she really never come with a friend?"

"Not while I've been here." She eyes the open window and her hand slides towards the cigarette packet. "Right, let me tell you about breakfast."

"You know," says Leonard, putting his elbow on the desk as though settling in for a good long chat, "we tried to get Willa to tell us exactly what it is that makes her come back again and again. So that we get the most out of our stay. I mean, it's unusual, isn't it, to come to the same place again and again. Is it the sausages at the breakfast buffet or the friendly staff or the tea rooms in a nearby village? Does she have a local friend? That was your guess, wasn't it, darling? Or a particular place she visits each time? What is it she does here, what is it that keeps her coming back and back —"

"Oh, there's no mystery to it." The receptionist has lost interest in them; the TV fades to black-and-white. "Every time she walks through that door she says exactly the same thing: 'My lungs have got a bit sticky and the doctor's prescribed a few days of good clean Norfolk air to clear them out.' Then she sits in the garden doing her thing and that's it. I always tell her she's crazy to breathe London air seven days a week if her lungs are bad." She opens a new game of solitaire on the computer and takes out a cigarette. "Breakfast is between seven and nine in the big room down that corridor," she says quickly. "Don't forget to sign the guestbook at some point, and if you have any questions at all, just pop down and see me."

THE WAITER

"My good man," says Leonard to the teenage waiter, dialling up his Yorkshire accent to pantomime proportions, "what do you recommend? I could eat a horse. Do you serve horse?"

"Chef's special is the sweet-and-sour pork."

"Chef's special, eh? When I was your age I worked in a place like this and at the start of each shift the chef used to say to us" – he lowers his voice to a whisper – "'I'll tell you what we need to offload and whenever a guest asks for a recommendation, tell them that. Call it the chef's special.' His words exactly."

"Oh, well…" The waiter giggles nervously. "Everyone says it's really good. Even the Chinese lad who washes the pots, and he should know." The profound gloom of the restaurant can't obscure the waiter's blush. It rises like damp from a white collar held loosely in place by a tie knot the size of a large onion. The only other diners are an elderly couple in the corner.

"How long have you been serving this sweet-and-sour pork of yours?" asks Leonard.

"I don't know. This is only my second week in the job." The acne on his cheeks glows red like hot coals, fanned by adolescent awkwardness. "Do you want me to ask?"

"I'm pulling your leg. Your word's good enough for me, young man. What about you?" Leonard asks Franny.

"A burger, please."

The sunlight pressing against the far windows is so dazzling that it seems all the surviving darkness in the world has crowded into this room to make its final stand. Leonard can smell hair gel and cut grass. In any operation, he thinks, there comes a time when you have to say out loud the thing you're there for, and however well you've concealed your intentions, the moment never fails to deliver a charge of electricity. "Your second week, eh?" he says. "Well, you're doing a great job. Our neighbour in London recommended this place. She comes regular as clockwork every three months, but I forgot to ask her what's good on the menu. You probably won't have met her if you're new, but it sounds like she knows everyone else. She's been coming here close to ten years."

"Ten years! She must like it."

"You'll meet her next week, that's when she's due."

"Oh, is she…"

"Is she what?"

"Nothing."

"Say it, lad."

He blushes again. "One of the boys said there's a regular coming next week who's a big tipper. He said he always carries her things out to the garden and she gives him a tenner. He told me to stay away."

"A tenner, eh? The gardens must be bloody big."

"She's got a bad leg," the waiter says, "is that her? Walks on a stick? I was wondering why she doesn't stay up the road at the hall. My cousin's girlfriend got a job there last summer and she says it's much fancier than this place. They've got a tennis court *and* a croquet lawn."

"I bet the staff are nicer here. No airs and graces."

"They're not allowed to chat with the guests up there, that's what I heard."

"That's what makes a place come alive for me, the people who work there. Tell me, though," says Leonard, "why did you say she should stay somewhere fancy?"

"Isn't she Lord or Lady something?"

Franny doesn't bother to hide her surprise. Outside, a man walks past the windows at a curious downward angle, his arms outstretched, as though slowly pursuing a child. It's only after he's gone from sight that Leonard smells the cut grass again and realizes he's pushing a lawnmower. "You know what," he says finally, "I think it's possible we're talking about two different people. What's your fancy lady with the bad leg called?"

"I only heard the others talking about her."

"Weren't you reading an article on the train about some fancy lady who lives near here?" he asks Franny. "Lady Williams or Winston or something like that? Chickens roaming through her house?"

"Peacocks," says Franny.

"Peacocks, that's it." He turns back to the waiter. "Is that her? Lady Williams?"

"No, this one's called … Lady Charlie, something like that."

"Lady Charlie?" says Leonard. "Come on, that's not a proper name."

"It's something like that."

"Have another go."

"I really shouldn't —"

"I'll tell the chef you've warned me off his sweet-and-sour."

"Lady Charlie," he tries again. "Lady Chatlie? Chattalake?"

"Lady Chatterley?"

"That's the one."

"I read something about her too," says Leonard. "So she comes here, does she, this Lady Chatterley?"

"I don't know." The waiter looks worried. "That's what the others say."

"She's definitely not our neighbour. Oh well, I hope you get a good tip from her. You'll get one from us, that's for sure." Leonard looks at the menu. "Now, have we ordered enough food for two extremely hungry people, do you think?"

"Would you like any sides?" asks the waiter. He wants to get away from this table. "Chips?"

"Doesn't it say somewhere on here that you grow all your own vegetables?" asks Leonard. "I think we'll share some buttered carrots." He hands the menu to the waiter. "Out of interest," he says, "what's the name of the gardener who grows all this lovely stuff?"

THE GARDENER

The man kneeling in the flower bed looks up at Leonard's approach, tilting his face out from beneath the wide brim of his straw hat. His teeth are neat and white against the brown of his skin.

"I've been admiring your handiwork," says Leonard. "These are beautiful gardens. At their best on a day like this, although it must be a struggle to keep everything watered."

The gardener is wearing brown trousers and a baggy white linen shirt. A red bandana is tied around his neck. The only clouds in the sky are faint, transparent wisps, loosely strung like fat on a carcass. The truth is that the gardens are beautiful, Leonard thinks, but unlike anything he has seen before. There's barely a straight line in sight, the hedges are untrimmed and although colour is bursting through everywhere he turns, the immediate effect is one of a landscape abandoned to its own chaotic ends.

"There's quite a few things I haven't seen before," says Leonard. "That maple back there – what's it called?"

"This one?" The man points with the trowel. "This one is a weeping maple. From Japan."

"I can imagine my parents might like one in their garden but I'm not sure whether it would survive in Yorkshire. What do you think? It's a bit brisk up there."

"They are strong trees, it will be fine."

"Do you put anything special on the soil?"

"No."

"And those silver birches," Leonard says, pointing. "It takes a while to realize they make a kind of pattern. Did you plant them yourself?"

"Yes."

"You've been here a long time then."

The man shrugs.

"And only one small lawn in the whole place," says Leonard.

"It is the most uninteresting part of a garden."

"I couldn't agree more. Well, I should be getting on. What's your name? I'll make sure to tell the manager how impressed I was."

"Ernesto."

"Ah, a Spaniard."

"Brazil."

"Have a nice day, Ernesto."

"Aha," says Leonard. "I was hoping I'd bump into you. Do you have any more of those little bottles of bath foam? My girlfriend likes to be completely hidden from sight. Fancies herself a bit of a Holly Golightly."

"Help yourself." She's in her early sixties, with a neat, grey perm and glasses on a silver chain around her neck. She tugs at the hem of a loose-fitting black dress with buttons up the front and lowers herself stiffly to one knee to inspect the underside of an upended hoover.

"Anything I can help with?" he asks.

"Oh, this happens every few days."

He takes two miniature bottles from the trolley. "Are you sure you won't get in trouble if I take these?"

"We've got boxes of them piled high in the store cupboard, no one's going to miss a few," she says into the bottom of the hoover.

"That's kind of you. I don't know how she can stand a hot bath on a day like this. A cold shower's the most I could handle."

The housekeeper sighs, puts on her glasses and begins to examine the brush, pulling loose a long clump of hair as tangled as a fisherman's net. Other treasures follow: a stone, dental floss, a sweet wrapper. She places her finds in a neat row on the pale green carpet.

"You must be near the end of your shift now," he says, leaning against the windowsill. "My mum worked in a hotel before she retired with bad knees. On her feet all day. It wore her out, plain and simple."

"Christ, you're a chatty bugger," she says. "Can't you see I'm busy? Your girlfriend's bath will be run over by now."

Leonard lives for moments like this one. There is the challenge of talking to a terrorist or a spy, but the challenge of talking to a cleaner with no patience and no time to spare is another version of exactly the same thing. "You've rumbled me," he says. "I've got an ulterior motive, you're right. I'm a reporter for the *Norwich Evening News*. I'm working on a story – a light-hearted piece, nothing more than that – about scandals behind the scenes of English country hotels. The grander the better."

"Pull the other one," she murmurs into the hoover.

"Don't let on to my girlfriend that we're having this conversation. It's our anniversary and I've had to swear to her I won't even think about work. But I've heard stories that there's some juicy bits and pieces going on here and I've got a wad of my editor's money burning a hole in my pocket that I'm supposed to be giving away."

"What nonsense you talk."

"There's a place near Cromer," he says, "fancy enough that it comes up in the Sunday supplements, where the sous-chef attacked the pastry chef with a meat fork, punctured his arse in two places. And I've got some missing petty cash in Fakenham, a waiter peeing in a fountain in North Walsham and rats in the kitchen in Sheringham." He counts them off on his fingers. "I've got a picture of that one. A rat the size of a cat. Literally. Paid a hundred pounds for it. But my editor says we need something saucy to complete the story. And I've heard a rumour that your gardener is a bit of a Lothario. Is that right?"

She straightens up, takes off her glasses and looks at him for the first time. It requires no special skill to read what she's thinking; suspicion, irritation and amusement are all visible in her expression. "Who did you hear that nonsense from? Don't pay it any attention – that's just the idle gossip of a few silly boys."

"I was hoping I'd stumbled upon the missing piece of my story. Are you really saying there's nothing going on? He isn't dipping his hose in the duck pond?"

A wad of chewing gum wrapped in a thick bundle of dust comes out of the hoover. He's got to be quick. If this happens all the time, she'll have it working again in a matter of minutes.

"Oh, shut up," she says. "He's friendly with one of the guests, that's all. Not with anyone else, that's for sure. And she's on sticks – there's not much anyone like that can get up to."

"If I've learned anything in my job it's that there's no smoke without fire."

"The handyman came round a corner one night and saw them sitting on a bench. There's your fire. It's those stupid boys in the kitchen who've spun it into something more. It's a sign of how bored they are. They're clearly not the only ones. But you're a grown man, you've no excuse." She rights the hoover and uses it to support her weight as she gets to her feet. "The only scandal around here is how much we're paid," she mutters.

"I can help with that," he says, holding out two twenty-pound notes.

"You're no reporter," she says, taking the money. "I don't know what you are, but you're not that. Handing out money for nothing at all. My nephew works for a paper in London and I've met plenty of the type."

"I promise —"

"You're in room seventeen, aren't you? Hasn't even got a bath, that one."

The hoover roars into life. The housekeeper rolls it over all the items she just picked out of the brush, turns abruptly and stalks off down the corridor.

Wednesday, 0011

The best cover stories require little explanation. The more you have to say, Leonard's instructors have drummed into him, the less likely you will be believed. So when they step out of their room, a few minutes after midnight, Leonard is wearing a dressing gown with a toothbrush tucked into the breast pocket for good measure and holding a mug containing a camomile teabag but no water, and in case it comes to it, which is very unlikely, he's removed the fuse from the plug of the kettle in their room. Franny is dressed in a pair of tracksuit trousers and a *Blade Runner* T-shirt. Her curly black hair is held back from her face by an eye mask. The greatest risk of being discovered comes from the ancient floorboards, more sensitive than any burglar alarm, and so their feet are bare. Leonard walked the corridor several times earlier that evening to see whether there was a route (edge versus middle) or a technique (at speed, on tiptoe, palms pressed against the walls to lighten his tread by a crucial pound or two, feet positioned diagonally to spread his weight over more than one floorboard) that might allow them to avoid the most screamingly loud creaks, but he couldn't find any pattern or consistency.

They start walking. The noise is deafening.

After three steps Franny pauses. "Shall I go back?" she whispers.

"Don't be silly."

They continue onward in darkness. The corridor lists so far to the right that the illuminated doorway ahead of them is closer in shape to a diamond than a rectangle. Once again Leonard has the sensation of being inside a sinking galleon; the floorboards call out beneath them like slaves in the hold. Franny is heavier than Leonard. When someone stirs in one of the bedrooms, she pauses again. "I'm going back," she says.

"We're not here to tiptoe," he says, reaching back to wave her onward. To his surprise, she takes his hand.

It feels like an age before they reach the carpeted landing. At some point – Leonard can't be sure exactly when – Franny lets go of his hand. They walk down one flight of stairs. Once they're in reception he switches on a table lamp and hands her the guestbook.

"Let's cast our net wide," he says. "I'd suggest one week either side of the dates of her visits. If there are any names that recur, cut out the page and we'll take it back to check for fingerprints." He stands up to go.

"I've had a thought," she says. "About the office."

The plan is that he'll go to room nine, where according to the receptionist Willa always stayed, and either pick the lock or force it open. He's not worried about a little splintered wood. It probably won't be discovered for a day or two, considering how few guests there are, and even then it'll be written off as accidental. No one will suspect a guest of breaking into an empty room.

"I worked in hotels every school holiday," she whispers. "When you've got an office that needs to be accessed by lots of staff, they often choose something memorable as the code. Otherwise you have to remind people all the time and someone ends up sticking it on a Post-it note. In one hotel it was the first four digits of the phone number, in another it was the number of bedrooms."

"I can see the logic," he says.

"The receptionist said the house was built in 1634. She had that number on the tip of her tongue. It's just a thought."

"Worth a try."

"You could sound more impressed," she says. "I used my intuition to come up with that."

"Is that a new program you've downloaded?"

"Funny."

"If it works there'll be no end to how impressed I am." He stands there for a moment looking at her.

"What?" she asks.

"What?"

"You were going to say something."

"Once this is all over," he says, "will you let me buy you a drink?"

As a general rule, Leonard is a calm person. So he is taken by surprise when his heart, lightly stepping down the corridor of his chest, begins to stamp its feet, to rattle every door.

"Oh," says Franny finally, "I don't think..." She is quiet. "It's not that," she tries again, "it's just that —"

"I'm sorry," he says quickly. "I shouldn't have asked."
Just yesterday, he thinks, I told Remnant nothing must
be allowed to get in the way of the work. And now this. It
contributes to his sense that something about this operation is causing him to spin off at unexpected angles. "Let's
see if your intuition is right," he says, stepping towards
the office.

The code isn't 1634; it's 3416. Leonard lifts the key from
the board and walks quickly to room nine without looking
back. It's a small, square room, dominated by a double bed
with a wicker headrest. There is enough light from the
windows for him to see what he's doing – it's one of those
summer nights when the earth has soaked up so much sunlight during the day that darkness never really takes hold.
Three porcelain geese fly in formation up one magnolia
wall and a large watercolour painting hangs above the bed.
A built-in wardrobe contains a shelf with two blankets, a
clothes rail, three hangers and a folding suitcase stand.

Leonard eases the casement window open and pulls
himself into a seated position on the deep wooden sill. It
would be possible – if a little difficult – to squeeze himself
through and lower himself into the garden, but he can't
imagine Willa doing it. Besides, he thinks, it would run
contrary to her habit of relying on a solid cover story, like
a walking stick and a well-timed cough. If she needed to
slip out after hours to meet someone, she would simply
add insomnia to her list of imaginary ailments and walk
out of the front door.

He sits on the bed. It's a relief to be on his own. It's a
relief to be on his own after what just happened. He's not

sure where to look next. The hooting of an owl calms him. Leonard feels a proximity to Willa here that takes him by surprise. It's partly physical, that he is in the room where she spent so many nights, where she was somehow more herself, where she was the secret self that for whatever reason she had chosen to become. But the exchange with Franny has thrown him into turmoil, and in his current state of vulnerability Leonard also detects in himself an emotional proximity to Willa, as though they overlap in some way, or as though he is wrapping himself in her feelings in the same way he wrapped himself in her coat, as though he has understood for the first time that he too is a traitor. He wonders when she realized that's what she was, and whether she felt fear or regret, or a surge of courage as her recruiter placed before her a choice, the latest in a series of small choices, each one presented as insignificant and inevitable but slowly lifting her further away from solid ground like the porcelain geese on the wall opposite.

Taking them down, he turns them over with trembling hands. His attention turns to the watercolour painting above the bed. It depicts the hotel from the direction of the pond. There's no signature, which strikes him as unusual. He remembers the receptionist saying Willa sat in the garden for hours "doing her thing", and the waiter said his friend had been given a tip for carrying "her things" out for her. Her things: could one of them have been an easel? Leonard's mind, trained the way it is, immediately sees the operational value in this, that in presenting the hotel with a painting she would have staked her claim to the place – to this room, where the painting is hung. It is a way of making it *her* room. Does that mean the room *is* significant? There's no way she'd leave anything important here, however well concealed, with the risk that another guest would come across it. Was it simply that the room provided a fixed vantage point from which to observe a signal? If she was given a different room each time it would be difficult for her handler to message her discreetly. Leonard looks out at the gardens, wondering what that signal might be, wondering if it is the sharp silvery glint of an abandoned spade, the cluster of earth-red plant pots, the single chair propped against the high, curved drystone wall. His mind returns to the picture. There were no paints or brushes in Willa's London flat. Where did she keep them?

He locks the room and returns to the front office. It only takes a minute to find what he's looking for. Franny comes in to see what he's doing just as he slides it out from behind a filing cabinet. He holds it up for her to see: a wooden easel and an A3-sized burgundy leather folder secured with a tiny padlock.

Back in their room they take the easel apart.

"There's nothing obvious in the guestbook," Franny says. "There's the initial 'W' next to a bland comment in June 2015. I've cut out that page and the ones either side, as well as a handful of other random pages to obscure what I was doing. But there are no recurring names around the time of her visits." She snaps the padlock on the folder with a pair of pliers. "About earlier," she says. "It's not that —"

He cuts her off with a gesture more blunt than he intends.

"Leonard," she says. "I don't think you —"

He gently takes the folder from her hands and turns it upside down. A dozen or so pencils of different lengths fall out. Then come a paint set and a bundle of brushes held together with a rubber band. They spread pieces of paper across the bed. There are several landscapes: fields, a tree covered in white blossom like snow, a village church, storm clouds. Willa has covered one sheet with at least a dozen small, precise sketches of flowers. But it is a notebook that interests them most. On every page is a drawing of a man – the same man. His features are lightly sketched and on their own hard to make out, but the wide-brimmed straw hat and bandana around his neck remove any doubt as to who it is.

"The gardener," whispers Franny, struggling to keep her voice down. "The gardener is her handler. You were right. The gardener is a Russian illegal. And he's still here."

Yes, thinks Leonard. It certainly does look that way.

But he is confused. Once again he is confused. It is possible, he thinks, that some of the sketches might have been made without the gardener's knowledge. But in others he is looking directly at Willa – he is *posing* for her. Assuming these pictures were drawn from life and not figments of her imagination, the gardener *knows* he is being drawn. That much seems clear. And the question Leonard is asking himself, given the intense levels of secrecy and caution required for a Russian illegal to have operated here for so many years, given the imperative every handler feels to remain in control of their agent, given the rigorous tradecraft and exhausting paranoia and importance of keeping up his guard every minute of every day – the question Leonard is asking himself is this: why on earth would a Russian illegal running an unimaginably valuable agent behind enemy lines contemplate *for a single second* the idea of allowing that same agent to draw a picture of him?

Wednesday, 1046

"Hello there," calls Leonard, striding across the garden. The temperature has climbed into the mid-thirties and the sun is burning a hole in the sky. He hears birdsong, a couple arguing as they walk to their car, the crunch of dead grass underfoot. The lawn crisps at its edges like a pancake. "You haven't found any money in the gardens this morning, have you?"

Ernesto stands up, wipes his hand on a rag and surveys the pieces of the lawnmower spread out on the grass around him. He is a short man, no more than five foot five. Leonard puts him in his early sixties. He lifts a wide-brimmed straw hat to mop his forehead and reveals a hairless, nut-brown head. There is a courtesy to the gesture that shows itself to have been unintentional when he barely turns away to spit. "No," he says.

"It's a bloody nuisance," says Leonard. "Will you let me know if you do find anything? It's quite a lot, one hundred pounds in twenties. Hard to miss if you come across it."

Ernesto looks briefly at him, nods once and turns his attention back to the lawnmower. The pieces are laid out methodically as though in a diagram. He is wearing the same baggy white linen shirt and brown trousers, secured

122

through the belt loops by a piece of grey rope tied in a bow at the front of his stout belly. His forearms are tanned and strong-looking.

"My girlfriend swears she left it in our bedroom, but she can be very absent-minded. What I *suspect* happened is that she dropped the money somewhere in the gardens this morning when we came out for a walk. But it's impossible to talk her out of an idea once she's got it planted in her head."

"If I find anything I will take it to reception."

"I'd appreciate it," Leonard says. "She's on the warpath and I worry it's going to spoil the whole day. And not just hers, if you know what I mean." He steps into the shade provided by a row of pine trees. "Looks like you've run into trouble there," he says, nodding at the lawnmower. It's an old model; some of the pieces show signs of having been soldered more than once. "Have you found the problem?"

Ernesto ignores him. There's enough of a breeze high up to sway the tops of the trees, but at ground level there's an enormous stillness. Everything is holding its breath – this heat can't last.

A drystone wall curves around the edge of the garden. Everywhere there are signs of precision, of careful, patient labour, of something constructed over a lifetime. Leonard looks at Ernesto. This could easily go wrong. He will need to exert pressure, but it must be no more than the pressure of a passing rainstorm, of the world going about its everyday business. "Look here," he says, "you haven't ever heard of money being stolen from the guest bedrooms, have you? If you don't mind me asking."

Ernesto looks up, surprised at the change in direction. His face is round, his large eyes a deep brown, his mouth long and expressive. "No," he says.

"The only reason I ask is that when we came back from our walk one of the chaps from the kitchen was hanging about in the corridor. Chinese, is he? Or Vietnamese? Something like that. Anyway, he looked … shifty. I can't imagine what he was doing up near the guest bedrooms. My girlfriend has got it into her head that he slipped into our room and stole the hundred pounds." Out of the corner of his eye he sees a crane rise off a branch and circle slowly down to the edge of the pond. "Do you know him at all?" asks Leonard. "Is he trustworthy?"

"I don't know him." Ernesto's eyes stay on Leonard. "Maybe you should speak with the hotel manager about this."

"I want to check the gardens first. My girlfriend's going through everything in our room. So we don't end up looking like bloody fools."

"As I said, if I find anything I will give it to reception."

"That's kind of you," says Leonard. "It's better for everyone if this doesn't escalate. She's capable of making a huge fuss, trust me."

Ernesto takes a red bandana from his pocket, dips it in a watering can and wraps it around his neck. As he goes down on one knee to continue his work on the lawn-mower, he says, "Do you think she will call the police?"

"Oh no," says Leonard. "She won't go to the police. We called them about a burglary at our flat last year and they didn't do anything. Completely hopeless."

Ernesto wraps a rag around the end of a twig and scrapes it around the neck of the fuel tank. He nods curtly in response to Leonard and adjusts the set of his shoulders to bring the conversation to a close.

"Her brother works in immigration, so she'll go down that route," says Leonard. "Restaurants are top of their list, then nail bars, then country hotels like this. That's what he says. You wouldn't believe how much is going on right under our noses. When they get a tip-off they pile in, go over everyone's papers with a fine toothcomb. If there's the smallest thing wrong with that Chinese lad's documents, or anyone else working in the kitchen for that matter, they'll be chucked out of the country in a flash."

Startled by a distant noise, the crane takes off, beginning its impossibly slow ascent to a vantage point high up on a nearby branch.

Ernesto peers into the fuel tank to see what's causing the blockage. He is in no rush. Finally he looks up at Leonard and squints. "The hotel manager makes sure everyone has the proper papers," he says. "Other places might be different, but here they check very carefully."

"I'm sure you're right."

"How will this help her get the money back?"

"It's not about the money," says Leonard. "It's more about the justice of the thing. That's how she sees it. And a bit about her temper, to be honest with you. She's quite right wing on these matters. I'm much more middle of the road – I think in some ways the country's been improved by foreigners. Curries, cricket, football. But it's often the way with the children of immigrants that they want to pull up the drawbridge behind them."

"This is a shame. Just because he is Chinese."

"Oh, she's not racist or anything – her dad's from the Middle East. It's more a political thing. She just hates the idea of people slipping in here under the radar and taking British jobs. If he's got the correct paperwork he'll be fine. That's it in a nutshell – at the end of the day, if he's got nothing to hide he'll be fine." Leonard takes out his handkerchief and wipes his forehead. He pulls his shirt away from his chest. "I really must go. You've got work to do. I'm only delaying because it's so nice to stand in the shade for a bit."

"This is a very severe measure to take if he did not steal the money."

"How thoughtless of me," says Leonard. "When I said all that about foreigners coming over here and taking British jobs I certainly didn't mean you. My girlfriend and I were both saying this morning how beautiful the gardens are. You're from Brazil, have I remembered that correctly?"

"Yes."

"Which part?"

"You know Brazil?"

"Not particularly."

"A small place near São Paulo, not many people have heard of it. But I have lived in many different places."

"Is that where you learned your trade as a gardener?" asks Leonard.

"No, I came to England a long time ago with a girlfriend,

we broke up and I needed to find a job. Twenty years later, here I am."

"And have you found a good Englishwoman to marry during that time?"

"What is it they say? I am married to my job."

"Well, I can tell you that my good Englishwoman is giving me a proper headache today, my friend, so I envy you your freedom." He watches Ernesto wash out the fuel tank with water and empty it on the grass. "If only women were as straightforward as lawnmowers, eh? If only there was a manual. Right, I'd better continue my search. Good luck."

Ernesto picks up a screwdriver. "Before you go," he says, "do you think you could help me?"

Leonard kneels beside him. They lean over the broken machine as though praying for its recovery. Ernesto puts the fuel tank back in its place and takes hold of Leonard's hands, gently lifting them onto the fuel tank.

"Keep still," he says.

He finds the right screw from a selection laid out on a small square of oily cloth and begins to secure the tank in place. Sweat from their foreheads splashes together on the metal.

"You can help her see reason," Ernesto says, starting on the second screw. "From what I have seen of him, he is just a young man trying to make a living, working hard, saving what he can, sending the rest back to his family. If you knew for certain he had stolen the money, I would call the police myself. If you knew he was here illegally, I would say good luck to you. But he is probably an honest

127

man, and it would be a shame if he came to hate this wonderful country that is so famous for its kindness and generosity."

He tightens the final screw and jumps to his feet, extending a hand to help Leonard up. Leonard takes it, laughing – he's not sure why. It's excitement, partly, and relief, but there is fear mixed in there too. Because if this man was Willa's handler, which he is now as certain of as he has ever been, then he was also her executioner. Does he know she's still alive? Does he know how close he is to being caught?

Ernesto smiles. "You will explain this to her?" he says, wiping his hands on his brown trousers.

"No chance," says Leonard. "I'm not sticking my head into the lion's mouth. The only thing that'll make her see reason is those five twenty-pound notes. Cheerio now." He sets off across the lawn.

"Wait," Ernesto calls out. "Wait. Which part of the garden did she walk in this morning?"

FROM THE ARCHIVES

3A

NOT PROTECTIVELY MARKED

MI5 Museum
Text accompanying exhibits 37–43

The Portland Spy Ring

In 1960 MI5 received a valuable tip-off when the CIA reported that the KGB had recruited a British official named Harry Houghton. A4 surveillance of Houghton, who worked at the Underwater Detection Establishment (UDE) at Portland, observed him meeting with a man named Gordon Lonsdale on a park bench near Waterloo Station (exhibit 37). Subsequent investigation revealed that Lonsdale was in fact a deep-cover Soviet agent known as an "illegal", and that his real name was Konon Molody (exhibit 38).

A Branch purchased a small attic flat near Regent's Park to use as a base for surveillance operations against Lonsdale. In the following weeks, officers watched closely as Lonsdale went drinking in the Duke of York pub (exhibit 39), stored packages in a safe-deposit box (exhibit 40) and visited a bungalow in

Ruislip belonging to an antiquarian bookseller and his wife, Peter and Helen Kroger (exhibit 41).

The Krogers were later discovered to be Morris and Lona Cohen, a married "illegal" couple who had been acting as Lonsdale's technical support team. A radio transmitter was discovered under their floorboards five days after their arrest (exhibit 42).

Gordon Lonsdale was freed in a spy exchange with the KGB in 1964 (exhibit 43).

NOT PROTECTIVELY MARKED

3B

SUBJECT: Operational Training (officer G86555)
DATE: 3 June 2019

Dear Charles,

I know you don't want any official record of the modified Human Intelligence and Tradecraft (HIT) course we ran exclusively for Franny at your urgent request, but I thought it'd be worth setting out a few things in writing for your personal records.

Your greatest concern was that others in the office would learn that Franny had received operational training. I can reassure you that due to the unprecedented measures we put in place you can be confident this has not happened. A typical training course requires up to a dozen instructors and guest speakers and a wide range of live exercise scenarios across the UK and overseas. In stark contrast to this, Franny's course was delivered entirely by one instructor working outside of normal working hours (evenings and weekends), meaning that Franny was able to perform her duties as a data analyst as normal during the daytime to avoid raising any suspicions. Instead of drawing on our cadre of undercover police officers to play the role of targets, we adapted our scenarios to use unsuspecting members of the public. We hired hotel rooms for the classroom sessions using a clean alias and paid for them with cash.

For these reasons Franny has not been tested in the same way or to the same degree as other graduates of the course, and there will be rough edges that need attention going forward. While the majority of these will take care of themselves, it is worth making you aware that Franny sometimes struggles to keep her emotions in check. Something we seek to develop in our students is the ability to harness their natural energies, enthusiasm and character while suppressing any personal opinions or feelings that might impede the building of rapport with an agent, and there were times on the course that Franny found herself drawn into an argument with a notional agent because she was simply unable or unwilling to let an objection-able comment pass by. While such strength of character and principle is admirable in a member of the public, it can limit a spy's ability to dissemble and exploit in ways unfortunately required in this day and age.

I do not believe you should let this deter you from using Franny on your operation. She was a conscientious and bold student, displaying at every stage of the course a compelling blend of warmth and character, and I am happy to report that by any reasonable measure she is able to deploy operationally.

In a private moment, Charles, you confided in me that the target you intend to deploy her against is skilful, devious and possibly even dangerous if cornered. Franny possesses the natural attributes and now also the operational skill set to enable her to work against such a formidable individual, and we are pleased to have been given the opportunity to contribute to what is undoubtedly an extremely important operation.

T. Gastrell

Head of Operational Training

TOP SECRET

3C

Staff Intranet: Blogs

Charles Remnant introduces us to his favourite pastime

I was delighted to be asked to contribute to this series of "blog posts" in which senior officers share details of a personal passion. Having heard in recent weeks from Clive about his love of Handel and from Lucinda about the martial art of karate, it is my turn to tell you about the ancient practice of apiculture, better known as beekeeping.

Some may see it as fitting that the head of Gatekeeping should identify with a creature that is committed at all costs to the defence of its home, that is passionately loyal to its Queen and that most people do their best to avoid out of an irrational fear of the occasional nasty prick. But the truth is that honeybees (*apis*, to give them their Latin name) are social creatures that are among the most organized and industrious in the natural world, responsible not just for the production of honey but also for the ingredients that go into candles, soap and lip balm.

Did you know, for example, that the honeybee performs what is known as a "waggle dance" to communicate information to its peers about nearby sites that are rich in pollen or might be suitable for new nests? Or that the entrance to a hive is protected by a small number of bees that detect and deter strangers who may pose a threat? Even the beehive has a Gatekeeping team!

The history of beekeeping is no less fascinating, turning as it does on a single discovery in the 19th century by a man named Lorenzo Langstroth. He found that bees left to their own devices will always leave a gap of between 5 and 8 mm between honeycombs that they do not block with wax, using the space instead as a passage for movement. This discovery led Langstroth to design a hive that accommodated the bees' natural habits and yet allowed the beekeeper to slide out the frames without disturbing the important work going on within. To carry out his inspections, which are vital to ensuring the well-being, productivity and stability of the community, the beekeeper will often use smoke, as it interferes with the production of the bees' alarm pheromones and "tricks" them into acting cooperatively.

In case this has whetted your appetite, I will be in the restaurant every morning this week selling honey from my own hives for the very reasonable price of £5 a pot or £1 a "drizzle" for your cup of tea or bowl of porridge. All proceeds will go to a charity that promotes the awareness of mental health issues among young men. Do pass by to say hello, have a chat and ask any questions you like – despite our reputation, we do not sting! Please also remember that we provide a friendly, sympathetic and discreet ear if you have any concerns whatsoever about the probity of your colleagues.

Charles Remnant

Head of Gatekeeping

CONFIDENTIAL

CHAPTER FOUR

Thursday, 0844

1

"Let me make sure I've understood you correctly," says Remnant.

The hot weather has broken and rain volleys like gunfire against the reinforced glass window of his rooftop office. Leonard is in no hurry. He was awake all night and arrived early this morning, more than an hour before Remnant. Standing in the corridor outside, opposite broken safes and metal cabinets lined up like the ramparts of a castle wall circling Remnant's high, airless kingdom, he thought: where does Remnant *come* from? There's nothing personal on display in his spartan room, so he must have an office elsewhere in the building, one with a computer, a desk, a teacup and saucer, a hook on which to hang his raincoat, a picture of the Queen, a telephone that rings when his wife wants to know which train he's planning to catch. Remnant's real life must happen elsewhere, Leonard thinks, which for some reason feels like a second-hand observation until he remembers that he concluded much the same thing about Willa and her flat a few days earlier.

"The gardener handed a single twenty-pound note to the receptionist," Remnant says, "appropriately crumpled and smeared with mud, which he claimed to have found near the duckpond. A smart move, operationally speaking. It would have been far too convenient to pretend he'd found all five twenty-pound notes. But finding just one allows for the possibility it came from elsewhere, that it wasn't Franny's money, in case the whole thing was a ruse to lure him into the open. As a Russian illegal, if that's what he is, he must be alive to that possibility every moment of every day. At the same time, he hopes twenty pounds is enough of a clue that she dropped the money in the garden to dissuade her from calling the immigration hotline."

The wind is blowing so hard that the rain streams against the window in crooked diagonals. Remnant watches it approvingly. His tweed is more suited to this weather. His good eye flickers as it tracks a rivulet down from the top right corner.

"What does this tell us?" he asks. "That the gardener is worried about the immigration status of a Chinese man he doesn't know? Unlikely. That he's worried about his own immigration status, as are many people? Possibly. Or that he fears an inspection by the authorities will reveal something amiss, something more than an expired visa or a lapsed work permit, something that suggests he's an illegal operating under an assumed identity? As thorough as the Russians are, it must be a constant worry for them that something in the paperwork trail will give them away."

The building is supposed to be airtight, but Leonard can hear a draught rustling the piece of paper that reads ELECTRICAL EQUIPMENT: STRICTLY NO ADMITTANCE on the other side of the door.

"Then we come to Willa herself," continues Remnant. "She has visited the same country hotel every three months or so over a period of at least ten years, and justifies this by claiming to have been told by her doctor that she needs regular doses of fresh country air – something her medical records suggest is untrue. She further bolsters her cover story by pretending to require the aid of a walking stick. There are rumours among the hotel staff that she's having an affair with the gardener, and a few drawings in a sketchbook appear to confirm some sort of connection."

Remnant speaks slowly and deliberately, his eyes fixed on the rain-soaked window. Before he tells this story to others he will need to straighten the crooked diagonals of Leonard's account.

"Is the case strong enough?" he asks, drumming his fingers softly across the tabletop. In the corridor outside, the draught swings a cabinet door closed with a small metallic echo. "A defence might look like this: Willa knew that a close relationship with a foreign national of uncertain immigration status would disqualify her from working here and so she sought to conceal it from view. Why not resign and conduct the relationship in the open, you might argue. Why go to these lengths over so many years to keep it secret? But maybe she liked working here, maybe she valued the job security, maybe she simply needed the income. Some of what you've told me,

Leonard, I would file under the 'interesting but nebulous' category: the discrepancy between the character reflected in her home and the character perceived by her colleagues, her avoidance of accumulating personal items that might reveal too much about her, even your claim to discern something of the skill of the agent handler in the way the gardener tried to persuade you to talk Franny out of calling the immigration hotline – none of these are in any way conclusive. You will be the first to recognize this."

For ten years Leonard has worked in a building that is physically sealed off from the outside world, and so the presence of a draught seems significant. It plays around his ankles and ruffles Remnant's flat grey hair. He is surprised Remnant hasn't felt it – Remnant, who takes notes when he overhears a piece of gossip, who looks askance at the woman who serves him coffee, who rides the lift stiffly like an antenna tuned to frequencies of anxiety, frustration and guilt. Or maybe he *has* felt it. Of all people, given everything he knows, maybe Remnant is acutely aware of every draught and every crosswind, maybe he alone knows the full extent of the storms bearing down on the building from all directions. Maybe it's Leonard who has woken up to the weather.

Remnant turns to face Leonard. He has come to a conclusion. "Acknowledging that gaps in understanding will always exist in our line of work, Leonard, it is nonetheless evident you have put together an extraordinarily compelling case. The measures Willa took to conceal her relationship with the gardener were clearly examples of professional tradecraft. It is very difficult to accept that they were employed so rigorously and over such a long period merely to protect a romantic liaison. Furthermore, your little ruse with the money showed him to be desperate to avoid the scrutiny of the authorities. Add to the mix the fact that Willa has been poisoned with a substance we cannot identify and the fragment of Russian chatter about an English oak being felled, and the case is as overwhelming as one can reasonably expect in the circumstances."

He pauses to see Leonard's reaction: there is none. This doesn't mean nothing is happening. Leonard's mind is working furiously. He still can't decide which way to go, despite having spent the whole night thinking about it. He has concluded that this operation is a puzzle that can be pieced together in two completely different ways, producing two completely different images. He has never come across such a thing before. What is remarkable is that both images are logical, coherent and recognizable; even under a microscope there are no lines that don't meet, no bruised cardboard edges. And so it becomes simply a question of deciding which image is more consistent with his experience of the world.

"We are now faced with the appalling likelihood that one of our officers has been run as an agent by a Russian illegal for at least the past ten years, possibly longer," says Remnant. "This is a crisis on a scale unprecedented in recent times. But it is only right that before turning to that crisis I take a moment to salute your fine work. Everything I've been told about you is incorrect, Leonard, but only in the sense that it doesn't go far enough. To have been given the extremely challenging timescale of five days and to have delivered beyond expectation in four is remarkable. You have demonstrated imagination, persistence, cunning and operational skill to an exceptional degree. In due course, those at the top of this organization will want to congratulate you themselves, and although this case must never be discussed outside this room, you must let me know when you wish to apply for promotion so that I can ensure your performance as a Gatekeeper is taken into account in the appropriate way."

Rain blurs the window; it fizzes like a television with no reception. Remnant is talking quickly now.

"There's one last task to be carried out before you are released from your Gatekeeping duties. In your conversation with the gardener you chose to alarm him with the talk of an immigration inspection. This was a good tactic and one of which I wholeheartedly approve. But it seems to me there's a small chance he'll have been sufficiently alarmed to consider fleeing the country. Would you agree? Of course, we will stop him if he tries to do so. But we would much prefer that he remains in place so we can watch him closely to understand how he operates. I would therefore like you to return to the hotel, seek him out and reassure him that Franny has not and will not call the immigration hotline as she now accepts she lost the money in the garden. That will draw a line under the episode. Are these instructions clear?"

Leonard doesn't answer.

"We'd better bring this to a close," Remnant says. "I'd like nothing more than to chew over your accomplishments all morning. But I've got a long day ahead of me."

Leonard doesn't move.

"We'll have to talk to the Home Secretary," says Remnant. "It won't be an enjoyable conversation. Then there's the matter of arranging around-the-clock coverage of the gardener."

In an empty room like this Remnant is without the usual means of signalling his impatience. There are no papers to shuffle, there is no briefcase to pack.

"Get the surveillance teams out," he says, "install some bugs in his cottage. I'll set Franny to work examining his documents."

He looks at his watch and sighs.

"Leonard? You're being very quiet. Is everything all right? Do you want to ask me anything?"

2

He still can't decide which way to go. In one sense, Leonard realizes, it doesn't matter what the puzzle depicts. Now he has glimpsed the other way the pieces can be configured, the unforgettable image they combine to form, he has no choice but to see this through to the end. It will cost him his position as a Gatekeeper, that much is beyond doubt. It may even cost him his job.

"Leonard?" asks Remnant. "Are you all right?"

He is on the train, travelling back to London. Franny sits opposite. *Click* goes a railway switch far beneath them. With an almost imperceptible jolt they change direction. *Click. Click.* Leonard finds a book about birds in Willa's flat. Some of the pages are more worn than others. *Click.* Leonard finds an Oyster card in the pocket of a shirt hanging in the wardrobe. *Click.* Leonard finds a packet of half-eaten Norfolk fudge.

"Leonard? What's going on?"

Click. Franny retrieves an old phone record that leads them to a remote Norfolk hotel. He looks out of the window at the riotous splendour of the trees racing past the carriage window. Don't let anyone tell you a tree is green, he thinks. The truth is always much richer than that.

"Leonard? Do you intend to sit there all morning without saying a word? Leonard?"

A fair question. Time is passing. Or rather, time is looping, spinning, circling like the swallow that flies alongside the train. What are Leonard's intentions? To do the only thing he can do, to do it the only way he knows. "You asked whether I had any questions," he says, leaning forward in his chair. "I do have a couple, as it happens."

Remnant looks surprised.

"Am I right in thinking," Leonard says, "that there is no secret cadre of officers referred to as Gatekeepers, that you've known all along that the gardener was a Russian illegal, that the real target of this operation was me?"

3

"I've never heard anything so absurd," says Remnant. "Have you lost your mind?"

Leonard knows an exchange of this kind will have to be quick and bloody. If he's allowed too much time, Remnant will realize that to win this skirmish all he has to do is sit calmly astride his horse and keep his soldiers in formation.

"It's not really a question," says Leonard. "It's perfectly obvious from the facts. Maybe I should rephrase it. The real question is why you thought it was necessary to go to such lengths."

Remnant stares at him. "You must be exhausted," he says. "The pressure of these last few days has been enormous. Why don't you —"

"Willa's flat," says Leonard. "It was like a training exercise, the way you packed it with clues. What were you thinking? If you search a property on a training exercise, there's always something to find – it's like an Easter egg hunt. It's simply not like that in the real world. The two things are as different as scooping fish out of a barrel with a net and heading out to sea in a leaky boat with nothing but a hook and —"

"Easter eggs? Fish in a barrel? Leonard, what on earth are you talking about?" asks Remnant.

"I'm talking about a birdwatching book with some of the pages marked. No one at the hotel noticed during Willa's ten years of visits that she was a birdwatcher. But that's the book she chooses to keep by her bed."

"What has that —"

"I'm talking about an Oyster card with details of her journey to Liverpool Street in May," says Leonard. "It was in the pocket of a shirt that was dry-cleaned very recently, in fact a full month after the last journey it was used for. The dry-cleaner would have removed it – why would Willa put it back?"

He doesn't know if this is true. He doesn't know if Willa was or wasn't a birdwatcher either. But details are important. Good poker players know you don't bluff indiscriminately – you bluff a precise hand.

"I'm talking about the fudge," Leonard says. "According to the label it was bought *after* Willa's most recent visit to Norfolk. How is that possible? It's only possible because *you* put it there, along with the Oyster card and the bird-watching book. You knew there was a Russian illegal in Norfolk and you wanted me to think I had discovered him myself, so you scattered clues around the flat like giant breadcrumbs and stepped back to let me follow them. You're a desk man, Remnant. You think life is like an Agatha Christie novel. But you've no idea how these things work in the real world. That's probably how you lost your eye —"

"What? How dare you —"

"That's why you told me not to break anything in Willa's flat. It wasn't because there was a nosy neighbour downstairs, was it? It was because you didn't want me to discover the cameras you'd hidden in every room to watch me."

"I've never heard such utter —"

"If you wanted to ask me something, you should have just asked me a straight question. We're supposed to be on the same side."

"Get out," says Remnant. "Get out this —"

"I'm not going anywhere."

"If I need to call —"

"You can imagine how confused I was at first. I don't mind admitting it. After the trail of clues, what on earth would I find at the hotel? What would be waiting for me? But it was obvious in a second that the gardener is the real thing, that he isn't another amateur actor in your little charade. So the question becomes, why on earth did you deliberately guide me towards a Russian illegal living in the English countryside? As astonishing as it is, there's only one possible answer."

"And what's that?"

"I can't wait to release this story into general circulation, Remnant. I don't know which part of it to highlight, whether I should lead with the utter incompetence or whether it'd be more damaging to talk about the bullying, the harassment, the misuse of official resources, the corrosive effect of being suspected by an office I've served diligently for the last seven years. Given your track record, given the way people feel about such things these days, given the fact that I'm innocent, I'm not sure you'll survive. I heard rumours this would finally be your year for a Queen's Honour. Not any more, I'm afraid."

Remnant considers the situation. "You haven't said what you think this is about," he says quietly.

"You think I'm working for the Russians." Leonard settles back in his chair to see whether his raiding party has spilled enough blood.

4

"If I wanted to know something, why didn't I simply ask you a straight question? Is that really what you just asked me?" says Remnant to the window. He can't bring himself to look at Leonard. "You little shit. You have no idea. You stupid little shit."

A minute or so passes.

"Yes, yes," Remnant says impatiently, as though he's had enough of the voice in his head. "There is more to this than you have been told. When is that not the case in our line of work? When is *anyone* told *all* the facts? Those classifications on every single piece of paper in this building, the ones saying 'Secret' or 'Confidential' or 'UK Eyes Only' – what do you think those are if not signs saying 'Keep Out' and 'Mind Your Own Fucking Business'? Are you going to tell me you've worked here for seven years and you don't understand that? You think I don't trust you? Of course I don't trust you – I don't trust anyone. That's my job." He shakes his head in disgust. He shoots his cuffs. "That's my job," he mumbles. "That's my job."

Leonard starts to get up.

"Sit down," Remnant barks at the window. A military man to the end, he can accept that surrender is sometimes the correct strategic decision. But he will walk out with his shoulders back, with his head held high. "It is imperative that what I tell you stays in this room. Is that understood?" Accustomed to being obeyed, he doesn't wait for an answer. "I had no choice," he says. "I had no choice, do you hear me? This office is facing a crisis on a scale so unprecedented that it's difficult to communicate its magnitude. At one end of the scale, and only if we manage to contain the worst of it, I would guess a dozen or so senior officers will lose their jobs by the end of the year. But that's nothing compared to the other end of the scale, which will see this entire organization pulled down and a new one built in its place, free of the rot that has set in."

The draught has picked up. Remnant lifts a stiff hand in a salute towards his ruffled hair. Although he knows it is impossible, Leonard feels as though the building is swaying.

"When Willa was poisoned just over a month ago we launched an urgent investigation into every aspect of her life," says Remnant. "On day eight we found old CCTV footage of her boarding a train to Norfolk, and on day nine we tracked down the taxi company she used to take her from the station to the hotel. When we broke into their booking system, we saw she had been a regular visitor for over ten years. So we sent in officers posing as guests, set up a surveillance ring around the hotel and began to dig into the background of every single person who worked there. It was on day fourteen or fifteen that our gaze settled on the gardener, not because of anything particularly incriminating, you understand, but because we have gained a good understanding over the years of the techniques the Russians use when trying to hide their illegals among us. We can spot the signs, let me put it like that.

"At the same time we made another discovery, one just as significant, one that had been under our noses all along:

it was Willa who vetted Jonas Worth, August Drummond and up to a dozen other officers who have been accused of serious misconduct in recent years. How anyone didn't spot this, that she was the one factor common to all these cases, I don't know. Her managers certainly never connected the dots. Perhaps Gatekeeping deserves its share of the responsibility too. When we caught someone engaged in misconduct, we never tracked backwards to see how they had joined the Service. We assumed they had been recruited and vetted in good faith – we didn't consider for a moment that someone had recognized they were bad apples and deliberately let them in, which is what appears to have been the case."

He has regained his confidence. There is pride in the telling of this story, thinks Leonard – pride and delight. Remnant is like a surveyor who thrills to the discovery of damp because it confirms what he has been saying for years: that the world is rotten to its foundations.

"It seems the only person who realized something was wrong was one of Willa's colleagues," he says. "But instead of reporting it to us as he should have done, he simply made a joke about it in her leaving card, which is what first prompted us to look in that direction."

Cabinet doors creak and groan in the corridor like giant grey birds.

"Now we get to the heart of it," Remnant is saying. "If Willa was a Russian agent, what exactly did she do for them? She didn't have access to sensitive intelligence, so what did she do that would justify them sending an illegal – an extremely valuable resource – to look after her?

What did she do that would justify a meeting with her handler every three months? When we learned she had a track record of letting in bad apples we all jumped to the same appalling conclusion: if Willa didn't steal intelligence herself, was it possible she had approved applicants she believed were corruptible and therefore recruitable and used them to create a network of sub-agents able to report back to her?

"At first, no one wanted to believe it was even a possibility. It's too ... too big, too bold, too terrifying. Say for argument's sake that she let in twenty-five candidates over the course of a year. Twenty of those might be perfectly decent – just to maintain her cover. But the other five might be candidates in whom she detects a character flaw she can exploit. They might drink too much or have a gambling addiction, they might be reckless or indiscreet or have problematic political views. Remember that vetting interviews allow her to explore every facet of their characters and behaviours. Of that group of five, she might then recruit the one or two most capable ones as her sub-agents and forget about the rest, or keep them for a later date, or wait until their personal circumstances mean they are ready to be activated. She might have blackmailed them. She might have said she needed to ask them in detail about their work to check they were reliable employees. Someone else might have recruited them – her role might simply have been to let them into the organization. Who knows? Over time some of them would leave for their own reasons, some would be dismissed for poor performance and some – like Jonas

Worth, like August Drummond – would be found guilty of unrelated misconduct because they were temperamentally unsuited to the job in the first place and should never have been hired.

"How big might such a network be? Over the course of her career Willa has vetted close to seven hundred officers, two hundred and forty-seven of whom still work here. Is it conceivable that a dozen of those are her sub-agents? Yes, it is. What about two dozen, what about fifty? She must have been cautious and skilful, because no one ever reported her. But even the smallest estimate would mean the Russians could reach into any part of the Service at will. Even the smallest estimate would mean we have been totally, irrevocably and fatally compromised from top to bottom." He sits back in his chair. "Do you see the scale of the problem? Do you understand we had no choice but to do everything in our power to find out whether such a terrifying scenario was real? But how? Willa was in a coma and there was no way a Russian illegal would confess. If we approached him we would lose any element of surprise and he would simply leave the country.

"So we addressed the problem from the other direction. We tried to work out who was a member of her agent network. How, though? She didn't have any friends here, she wouldn't even go out for a drink with her colleagues. Do you remember I told you that the way we caught August Drummond was by asking a small group of highly trusted officers to use gut instinct to guess who among their colleagues was capable of betrayal? I said that August's name came *near* the top, which is true. But do you know whose name came *at* the top?"

"Wait," says Leonard. "Wait. *What?*"

"That was in 2015. It took us five minutes to determine that you weren't responsible for the things August Drummond had done. But a note was attached to your file indicating that we should keep a watching brief on you, given your colleagues' concerns. When Willa was poisoned, and when we learned that she had approved your vetting, we decided to start with you. We did the obvious things. We listened to your phone calls, we searched your flat, we followed you around. You asked what we've been doing for the past month. Well, there's your answer."

"Wait. Wait."

"Do you want to hear this or not? After ten days we realized there wasn't enough time for the long game. If you were one of Willa's sub-agents, it might be months before you actually did something. So we had to force your hand, we had to create an artificial situation in which you might reveal yourself. And the best way to do this was to put you in front of the Russian in the hope you would say something illuminating. I'm not denying we were desperate, Leonard, that we were out of conventional ideas. But we thought if you talked face to face with the Russian in a context you thought was private you might admit to being one of Willa's sub-agents, or you might ask him what had happened to her, or you might say you wanted to take her place at the head of the network, or you might try to blackmail him. You might say nothing at all to his face, but your behaviour might provide us with valuable hints as to your state of mind. So we told you that you'd been made a Gatekeeper, planted clues in Willa's flat that would send you to Norfolk, put Franny next to you to report back and settled in to watch carefully. You know the rest." His shoulders drop. "It goes without saying that you've cleared your name."

"Wait."

"Your performance *was* exceptional. I hate to admit it, because I don't like you one little bit. But we've had over a dozen officers working around the clock on this and they never found out about Willa's sketchbook or picked up rumours that she was having an affair with the gardener. You gleaned more from your peregrinations around her neighbourhood than we thought possible. I'm praising you – look, we're back where we started." Remnant's impatience has returned too. "Have I answered all your damn questions?"

Leonard has never before seen it so clearly. The military values he glimpses through the billowing cannon smoke of Remnant's manner are not the values of sacrifice, loyalty and courage. What he sees instead is the court martial, the firing squad. What he sees is a hatred of deserters, of pacifists, of doubters, of the simply terrified. Leonard wonders how many people have been pushed out over the years because someone like Remnant decided they weren't quite right.

"Oh yes," says Remnant. "There is one point I haven't addressed. Why didn't I simply ask you a straight question? Were those your words, Leonard?" He leans forward across the desk. "Is that what you do when you suspect someone?

Ring them up and ask if they happen to be a foreign spy? Or do you follow them around, listen to their phone calls, read their emails, break into their home, persuade their closest friends to betray them? You've had a mouthful of your own medicine, Leonard, it's as simple as that. And now you're sitting here complaining it tastes bitter. Well, complain all you want. Your pathetic sense of injured pride is nothing compared to the problem this office faces. There's a Russian illegal out there who holds the key to all this, and our only hope is that by watching him we can find out how thoroughly we have been compromised. So forgive me if I politely and humbly request that you wipe away your tears, pull up your socks, keep your mouth shut, get out of my office and go back to reassure him that the immigration raid has been called off. Or would you rather throw another bloody tantrum?"

FROM THE ARCHIVES

4A

SUBJECT: Willa KARLSSON's record

DATE: 27 May 2019

1. In light of concerns raised by the Gatekeeping team about Willa KARLSSON, we have been asked to conduct an in-depth review of her professional record as a vetting officer.

2. This Note For File addresses two questions. The first question – undoubtedly the more straightforward of the two – is to identify which officers vetted by KARLSSON have been found guilty of serious disciplinary breaches over the past 10 years. We have defined a serious breach as one that resulted in an officer's employment being terminated.

3. The list of officers who fall into this first category is as follows:

    > K77103: Set up an anonymous Twitter account under the handle @notsosecret007 that published 448 tweets over a 2-year period. Tweets increasingly made use

of sensitive (if not quite secret) information about senior government figures and national security policy, and even produced a monthly "column" that referred in a satirical tone to social events within the 3 agencies (e.g. the notorious Christmas party brawl of 2016). CPS lawyers advised against prosecution on grounds that the tweets caused "embarrassment rather than damage". Upon closure the Twitter account had just under 300,000 followers.

G66529: Decorated agent runner believed responsible for a series of security breaches including passing US intelligence to an unauthorized third party, planting drugs on a Russian diplomat and leaking the recording of a phone call between an Islamist cleric and a prostitute to a tabloid newspaper. Came to be known as the "Robin Hood case" because of the supposedly "ethical" nature of the breaches. Dismissed for assaulting a fellow officer.

G77298: Went off-script in a performance of the annual Service pantomime (on the night the Home Secretary and Justice Minister were in attendance) to sing an extremely crude song mocking a number of senior government figures. Resigned voluntarily the next day upon hearing she had been summoned to a meeting with Head of Gatekeeping.

K77103: Analyst who admitted stealing several hundred intelligence documents to use as ransom when his father was kidnapped by Islamic State in Syria. Was the target of a joint operation with the CIA in Beirut. Location of stolen documents remains unknown.

K42782: Complained to the Ethics Counsellor about links between British intelligence and oil/gas companies. Escalated the complaint by writing without permission to Parliament's Intelligence and Security Committee. Caught by security guards in the act of attempting to unfurl a Greenpeace banner from the roof of Vauxhall Cross. Currently working as "covert action organizer" for a climate change group.

A45521: Surveillance officer who developed addiction to alcohol as a result of work pressures. Involved in a serious physical altercation with his line manager at a staff Christmas party in 2016.

4.   The second and significantly more challenging question is to ascertain whether there are officers a) vetted by KARLSSON b) *still* employed by the Service and c) whose professional conduct suggests they merit further intrusive investigation. This question is hard to answer with any certainty because of the difficulty in knowing exactly what we are looking for, as evidenced by the breadth of crimes and misdemeanours described above.

5.   The list of officers who fall into this second category is considerably shorter and follows below:

P38862: Counter-intelligence specialist whose name was put forward by a focus group in 2015 as being "more likely than his/her peers" to be working for a hostile foreign state. Currently the target of an extensive Gatekeeping operation.

J76730: Archivist of 32 years' service whose photo-copying habits have been flagged as unusual by a prototype algorithm looking for anomalies in staff technology use. Nothing else in his record to prompt concern, other than a 2003 request for permission to publish a novel, which was turned down. Surveillance of the archivist has been fruitless, and an initial search of his flat turned up nothing suspicious. A further search is planned.

F65572: Highly decorated investigator and recipient of numerous awards. Her personal internet usage indicates that she has purchased several books about the health benefits of hallucinogenic drugs, and travel records show she has visited California on four occasions over the past two years. A "random" drug test will be conducted in the next month.

G82331: Middle manager accused by a colleague in 2005 of leaking stories about American enhanced interrogation and other controversial techniques by discussing the topic loudly in Whitehall pubs known to be frequented by journalists. The allegation was not taken seriously at the time but will be followed up as a matter of urgency.

TOP SECRET

4B

FROM:	Behavioural Science Unit
TO:	Gatekeeping
SUBJECT:	Grave concerns
DATE:	6 June 2019

Charles,

I trust enough time has passed since our encounter in the cafeteria this morning to allow tempers to cool. If my words in any way contributed to the ugly tone that crept in towards the end of our conversation, I offer my sincere apologies. I hope we can now continue our discussion in a more collegiate manner.

To recap: we in the BSU are proud of our role in assisting investigative teams such as yours in their crucial work. A vital part of this is developing new methods. In this context, in 2015 we took a technique used by the CIA to identify the Russian agent Aldrich Ames and brought it up to date by running a highly covert and compartmentalized "focus group" of select staff to harvest views on who among their colleagues might be disloyal or disobedient. This process assisted Gatekeeping in their identification of August DRUMMOND.

Crucial to the success of this technique was the fact that it was used in conjunction with other investigative methods and not in isolation. As we cautioned at the time, the technique can provide valuable insights but is often unreliable because of the role played by unconscious or affinity bias. Used on its own, it is unlikely to tell you much more than who is and isn't popular. In some ways, therefore, it brings to mind the discredited "tap on the shoulder" recruitment system used for many years which led to our community being so unrepresentative of the wider population it serves, and which proved so ineffective at keeping out foreign spies.

It is for these reasons that I was extremely alarmed to learn you are mounting an investigation into a serving officer solely on the grounds that his name was highlighted by that same 2015 focus group. I cannot emphasize strongly enough that in our professional judgement this is a grave misstep, both ethically and in terms of the investigative outcomes you are pursuing.

M. Clutton

Head of Behavioural Science Unit

Dear Matthew,

Thank you for your email. As I tried my best to explain in the cafeteria this morning (I can only imagine you were distracted by the delightful smell of bacon and eggs wafting upwards from your crowded breakfast tray), the work of the Gatekeeping team is among the most sensitive carried out in the intelligence community. Since we only share information with those who need to be involved, I must admit it has taken me by surprise to learn that you are even aware of the operation you mention. For this reason, I would be ever so very grateful if you could let me know the name of the individual who informed you about it so that appropriate disciplinary steps can be taken.

Yours,

Charles

Charles,

I was hoping you would take this opportunity to engage in an honest dialogue with someone equally committed to and passionate about the effectiveness and security of this organization. Please understand that I have no wish to undermine your work or your position. Please also understand that although your work quite rightly takes place in secret, it nonetheless has an impact on the wider community of which we are both a part. It is therefore crucial that you are open to a conversation of this nature, just as it is crucial that I listen to others' views about the team I run.

To repeat my point, investigating a member of staff on the basis of nothing more than the idle speculation of their colleagues is a highly dubious practice, both operationally and ethically. I have also been made aware of a Gatekeeping investigation into an archivist on the basis of a lead generated by a prototype algorithm that I am told is untested and likely to produce results of uncertain reliability. How can these two operations be justified?

I am not going to give you the name of the person who supplied me with this information. Please address the points I raise.

Matthew

FROM: Gatekeeping
TO: BSU
SUBJECT: Re: Re: Re: Grave concerns
DATE: 6 June 2019

Dear Matthew,

As you point out, the "focus group" technique is not one you created. Rather, it is one used by the CIA in the 1980s and undoubtedly other organizations over the years. It is sweet, and more than a little amusing, that you believe you have ownership of it as a technique, but of course this is not the case, and you have no right to tell me what to do or what not to do in the investigations that I run.

Needless to say, I am highly concerned to learn that you have been told about a second Gatekeeping investigation, as this suggests we have a serious problem to address. I am not able to divulge any details of that second case but would ask you to consider, before you throw around such ill-advised accusations, the potential damage caused if an officer with access to our archives started making that material public.

Once again I ask, what is the name of the person who leaked details of our operations to you?

Charles

FROM: BSU

TO: Gatekeeping

SUBJECT: Re: Re: Re: Re: Grave concerns

DATE: 6 June 2019

I can see this dialogue is fruitless. I will take this up with your superiors.

Matthew

FROM: Gatekeeping
TO: BSU
SUBJECT: Re: Re: Re: Re: Re: Grave concerns
DATE: 6 June 2019

Matthew, my dear chap. Please take this up with whomsoever you wish. I trust they will point out to you something you seem to have forgotten, which is that this community you profess to love so dearly exists not to dispense warm hugs but to intrude covertly into the lives of others, some of whom will be innocent and some of whom will be guilty.

While you are being schooled by your masters in the ways of the world, I must continue to exercise my responsibility for the internal security of this organization. If you do not immediately provide me with the name of the officer who informed you about our operations, I will instigate disciplinary proceedings against you before the end of the day.

The last thing I wish to do is alarm a sensitive soul such as yourself, Matthew, but you should be aware that sanctions at my disposal include termination of employment, criminal charges and removal of accrued pension rights.

With my very best wishes,

Charles

4C

SUBJECT: Operational strategy

DATE: 10 June 2019

1. This document sets out the strategy for the three phases of Operation THUNDERCLAP.

Phase One: London

2. Leonard FLOOD (hereafter LF) will be allocated a flat in Regent's Park to use as a base for the duration of the operation. A full suite of covert monitoring equipment has been installed in the flat, allowing us to observe LF at all hours of the day and night.

3. While LF is staying in this flat, a team will carry out an uninterrupted search of his home address.

4. LF will be provided with the keys to Willa KARLSSON's (hereafter WK) flat and told to carry out a search. WK's flat has also been fitted with a full complement of covert monitoring equipment so LF can be observed

during the search in case he retrieves an item of significance.

5.   The following items will be placed in WK's flat prior to his arrival:

> A birdwatching book with Norfolk-related pages marked as though by frequent use
>
> A half-eaten packet of Norfolk fudge
>
> An Oyster card with record of recent travel to Liverpool Street

6.   If LF does not deduce from these items that WK regularly travelled to Norfolk, the following measure can be used at the discretion of the ops room manager:

> A phone call made to the flat while LF is present claiming to be from the Norfolk hotel and enquiring whether WK still intends to visit as planned

7.   Other than placing the items in WK's flat and possibly making the phone call purporting to be from the hotel, we will allow LF to act entirely as he wishes. He will be free to engage with WK's neighbours and any members of the public he chooses, and to visit any locations he wishes, in the hope that in doing so he reveals something to indicate he is aware that WK is a Russian agent. A surveillance team will be positioned around WK's flat to observe LF in the event he makes contact with individuals or travels to locations relevant to the investigation.

Phase Two: Norfolk

8. LF will be told that the deadline for his investigation has been brought forward. The purpose of this is to place additional pressure on him and increase the likelihood he will make a mistake.

9. LF will be encouraged to deduce from the items recovered from WK's flat that she was a regular visitor to Norfolk. He will be told that for safety reasons he must be accompanied to Norfolk by another officer (hereafter FS). Although FS has recently undergone operational training, she will claim to have no operational experience and so will place herself under the supervision and guidance of LF. Her real purpose, however, is to monitor LF and steer him in whichever direction we require.

10. To facilitate the discovery that WK was a regular guest at a particular hotel in Norfolk, FS will claim to have discovered a phone call made several years ago from WK's home landline to the hotel.

Phase Three: Hotel

11. The hotel is a challenging operational environment as we cannot control what LF does or who he speaks to. However, to enable LF to identify the Russian illegal, the following measures can be used at the discretion of the ops room manager *if required* and communicated to LF by FS:

    The notional discovery of a CCTV image of WK with the Russian illegal at a local train station (technical

teams have spliced genuine pictures to create a
blurred image in which they are both recognizable)

The notional discovery by FS near the gardener's shed
of a book with WK's initials inside

The notional discovery of a safety deposit box in a
London bank under WK's name that holds stolen
intelligence documents with the initials of the illegal
written by hand at the top

12. Once evidence pointing towards the illegal has been
established, FS will step back and allow LF to approach the
illegal alone. Extensive technical surveillance in the hotel
and its grounds will capture any conversations between
LF and the illegal for immediate analysis.

TOP SECRET

CHAPTER FIVE

Thursday, 1037

Leonard is packing his bag in the attic flat when Franny calls. "I was hoping I'd catch you," she says.

Dark rain attacks the windows. He tucks the phone under his chin, folds a shirt and puts it in his bag.

"I just bumped into Remnant. He told me it's all come out," she says. "Or rather that you guessed half of it and he filled in the rest. This might sound weird, coming from me, but I'm glad it's all been cleared up – I'm glad you've got the full story."

Leonard hasn't slept and suddenly feels light-headed; he places a trembling hand against the back of the built-in wardrobe to steady himself.

"I was feeling very uncomfortable towards the end," Franny says. "I just couldn't believe they'd found the right person."

There is a thin bulge in the faded floral wallpaper beneath his hand that feels hollow. He finds the edge of the paper and tears off a large crescent, enough to see that the exposed plaster is a slightly different grey to its surroundings.

"Are you there?" she asks.

"Yes." Leonard runs his hand over the discoloured

plaster. "We probably shouldn't talk about this on an open line, Franny."

"I'll be quick. I just want to say sorry. It must have been horrible for you to realize what was happening, that you were a suspect and this whole amateurish charade was intended for you."

"Amateurish charade?"

"Remnant said that's what you called me, an amateur actor in his little charade. He's had me removed from the operational register. He said I have to bear some of the responsibility for you seeing through it all, something about not being able to keep my emotions in check. If I want to work in the field again, I'll have to redo the full course, not just the abridged version they rushed me through. I can't say I blame him. Anyway, this isn't supposed to be about me."

"You were very good, Franny. The truth is that I made up most of what I told Remnant. If he hadn't backed down so quickly I was prepared to claim I'd spotted surveillance behind me. It was just a series of bluffs."

"That's very generous, after everything that's happened," she says.

Leonard taps the wall again, remembering the long professional history of the flat, a veteran in its own right, at the heart of technical operations over the decades against nuclear scientists, extremist financiers, communist sympathizers and even one of the first Russian illegals discovered in the UK. He runs his hand along the underside of the shelf and finds an extra metal bracket, now speckled with rust, added long ago to support something much heavier than clothes.

"One of the things I told Remnant on Monday was that nothing should be allowed to get in the way of the work," he says. "This has been a good test of whether I really believe that."

"And do you?" she asks.

The area of discoloured plaster would be about the right size to accommodate an old bulky camera of the kind he remembers seeing in the office museum. Assuming the flat next door has the same layout, the camera would have been pointed into its bedroom.

"Leonard?" she says. "*Do* you still believe it?"

"There's something about the ruthlessness of Remnant's plan I can't help but admire."

"You must feel bruised."

"We work in a bruising business," he says. "You've got to take the lumps."

Leonard steps into the living room and looks around. The signs are everywhere. A trail of plastic clips once used to hold a heavy electric cable has been left running above the yellowing skirting board, and behind a sunken arm-chair in the corner is a wooden box that long ago housed a piece of equipment pointed at a property across the road. The technicians have been careless, he thinks. All their artistry has gone into the other side of the canvas, the side seen by the target; the back is an unimportant mess of nails, wires and splintered wood.

"Listen," he says, "I've got to —"

"I know you have to go." She pauses. "Are you angry with me?"

He looks around, wondering where they have concealed

the cameras and microphones installed to monitor him. They won't be so easy to find. "Can you hear me?" he says aloud.

"Yes, Leonard," says Franny. "I can hear you."

But he's not talking to her. He runs his hand along the wall, up and down the doorjamb. He pulls back a corner of the thin carpet.

"Remnant told me how they'd come to suspect you," she says. "In the cold light of day it seems so stupid. I guess I'd assumed the operation was based on more than just the hunch of a few old-timers."

"We're back to intuition again, aren't we?" Leonard says. "After what I said on the train, it'd be a bit rich if I complained now that the hunches of experienced officers should count for nothing. If that many agents all told me they had a bad feeling about the same person I'd sit up and listen. In fact, I've probably run intrusive operations based on less."

He finds a loose floorboard under the carpet and lifts it to reveal a coil of wire taped to a joist. It's old, too; over the years mice have nibbled away at the plastic coating.

"Maybe it's time you changed your mind," Franny says. "They're supposed to be the best this country has when it comes to hunches, right? And they were completely wrong."

"Were they? They must have seen something. I don't know what the numbers were, but even if just five out of ten, for argument's sake, thought I had it in me to be a spy for the other side, that suggests there's something there – a quality I have, an attitude, perhaps a lack of something … healthy. For me to come top in Remnant's poll means *something*. I just don't know what exactly. The problem is that you can't take risks with a job as important as this one. There's no room to give someone the benefit of the doubt."

"But you've been so successful, Leonard."

"Maybe to be a good rat-catcher you've got to have something of the rat about you."

"I don't like the way you're talking."

Leonard replaces the carpet and stands up too quickly. His head spins. He has a sudden urge to get out of here. The flat smells of a thousand cigarettes. Years of suspicion and paranoia cover the walls like layers of old paper. He opens the balcony doors and breathes deeply while below him grey clouds pelt the city with rain. This feeling he has, this feeling of being unable to connect with other people – despite the evidence presented anew each day, Leonard never fails to wake up hoping to find he has escaped it, that it is a feature of his past, that he has finally stepped blinking into the open air of adult freedom, that today is the day he'll meet someone who doesn't make him feel there is something broken inside him. He shouldn't be surprised to find that today is not that day. Life repeats itself, after all, this is what he believes. We only exist as children, and spend the rest of our lives performing the same loop, like birds alongside a train, and we are wounded in the same place, and we crash to the ground again and again with the same banal finality. The only thing that changes is the patch of ground.

"Are you still there?"

"I don't know what you want me to say, Franny." He raises his voice to be heard above the storm. Rain soaks through his clothes. "I don't blame you for anything. You did the right thing. I don't blame Remnant and I don't blame the colleagues who thought it was me. You said as much yourself, that I've got a reputation for being difficult. Ask yourself who you would have chosen if they'd put the list in front of you."

"That's not fair."

"I didn't join to make friends."

"I really don't like the way you're talking. Will you come and meet me?"

"I can't, Franny, I —"

"Come on, you owe me a drink for guessing the code to the office door, remember?"

Far below him the park is a vivid green tear in the sodden grey fabric of the city.

"Leonard?"

"Did you really guess it?" he asks. "The code?"

"I don't know why I mentioned it." She's quiet for a moment. "One of the search teams found it taped underneath the reception desk."

On the street below, black umbrellas bob unevenly like leaves on a stream about to burst its banks.

"Why *did* Willa let me in?" he asks, stepping out of the rain. He is talking to the room as much as to Franny. "If my colleagues don't think I fit, isn't it likely Willa saw that same quality in me too, whatever it is? So why *did* she let me in? *Is* it because she was planning to recruit me as one of her agents? I bumped into her in the stairwell about a year ago. It was the first time I'd seen her in ages. She wanted to know what I was up to, where I was posted, whether I was enjoying the work. She suggested we have lunch together. She wanted to ask me something, she said, but I had to go overseas on a job the next day, and when I came back I heard she'd resigned. What was she going to ask me?" He steps into the middle of the room. "And what answer would I have given her?"

"Leonard, are you all right?" says Franny. "You sound funny. What are you saying? Are you going to —"

He hangs up.

He feels alive with threat like an exposed wire.

He picks up a chair and swings it at the wall.

CHAPTER SIX

Thursday, 1755

1

It's almost six o'clock by the time he finds Ernesto sheltering from the rain in an open lean-to used to store firewood. His green waterproof coat stops just above his ankles and on his head is a wide-brimmed straw hat fastened beneath his chin with a knot. He shows no sign of surprise at the unexpected arrival of a visitor.

"I'm glad I found you," says Leonard, raising his voice to be heard above the rain thrumming against his umbrella. "I was beginning to give up hope."

A camouflage-patterned rucksack sits on the ground by Ernesto's feet. Plants in jars, pots of varnish, weedkiller tins are lined up along a makeshift shelf at the back of the lean-to. Leonard discerns anxiety in Ernesto's stillness, in the rigidity of his long, expressive mouth and large, staring eyes. His face is like an overcrowded tray held by someone unsure of their footing. An old Belfast sink half-buried in the earth slowly fills up with rainwater.

"I wanted to thank you for returning the money to reception," says Leonard. "My girlfriend was embarrassed when she realized she'd lost it in the garden after all, especially after what she said about the Chinese guy in the kitchen. Needless to say she's not going to be complaining to anyone. It'll teach her to be a little more careful."

Ernesto considers this statement and nods once. Leonard's thoughts flow like rainwater into suddenly obvious channels: that this job is perfect for someone in Ernesto's position – the stealthy cultivation of new life, the nurturing of roots, a garden as the ultimate underground network. Any one of the seedlings on the shelf behind him would be capable of penetrating the strongest of defences. Leonard has nothing else to say. He has discharged his final duty to Remnant. He nods goodbye and is a step or two down the path when he hears Ernesto speak.

"You asked about the tree."

Leonard turns around. Ernesto has come out of the lean-to. Rain bounces off the wide brim of his straw hat.

"A Japanese maple," he says. "Your parents would like one, this is what you told me." He gestures towards the shelf behind him. "I have a cutting. If you like, they can see if it will survive the cold weather where they live."

"That's very kind of you."

Ernesto turns and begins to look among the jars. "It must be in the greenhouse," he says. "Come with me." He picks up the rucksack and swings it onto his back. Without waiting for an answer, he walks past Leonard and down a narrow path of sodden woodchips that twists beneath a row of pines to emerge at the edge of the lawn. The hotel is no more than fifty metres away, but rain blurs its edges so it seems to be standing in mist. An orange light burns above the front door.

They walk along the edge of the lawn and pass through a metal gate into a kitchen garden planted in neat rows. Ernesto leads him through another gate into a small apple orchard, and as they walk he slows momentarily to inspect a leaf and rest his open hand against the bark of a tree. The earth has been so parched of water over the summer that despite the rain it is still firm underfoot.

In the distance a greenhouse comes into view. It is at the edge of the property, long, narrow and with a sloping roof built onto a stone wall at least ten metres high. In places its white wooden frame is black with rot. Dark indistinct shapes swirl against the glass. Ernesto takes a key from the gutter above the door and ushers Leonard inside.

"You'll have to give me some instructions to pass on," says Leonard, closing his umbrella, shaking it dry, leaning it behind the door.

"Instructions?"

"For the maple. Water, sunlight, compost – that sort of thing."

"Oh yes," Ernesto says. "For your parents."

The stone wall runs along one side of the greenhouse and on the other a long trestle table filled with plants has been pushed against the glass. Rain is dripping through the roof in at least three places.

Ernesto locks the door and wipes his face dry with a bandana from his pocket. "We need to talk," he says.

Oh, thinks Leonard.

"You are simply doing your job," Ernesto is saying. "It will give me no pleasure to hurt you. But a trapped animal is a dangerous animal, you must understand this."

Leonard's eyes go to his umbrella; Ernesto widens his stance.

"A trapped animal?" asks Leonard. "What are you talking about? Which one of us is trapped?"

"I don't have time for games."

"You're the one who's just locked the door."

"You're the one with a surveillance team surrounding this hotel. Where are they? What are your intentions?"

Leonard looks around. He considers a crack in the glass, the weight of a plastic pot. He looks for a trowel.

Ernesto burrows in his rucksack and produces a large, black, antique revolver.

"What?" says Leonard, lifting his hands. "Wait, what are you doing with that thing?"

"It was only as I was standing at the reception desk with the money in my hand, explaining I had found a muddy banknote beside the duckpond, that I realized you had lured me into the open." The revolver hangs from his hand. "And when I told the lady who the money belonged to, can you guess what she said? That you and your girlfriend are Willa's neighbours in London. Since then I have been noticing things I should have noticed a long time ago. Footprints in the woods behind my cottage, a city car parked in a lane that leads nowhere. I have been wondering why a pigeon abandoned its nest in the roof above my workshop. Now I know. All I need is a head start. Tell me how many of you there are and where they are positioned."

"This is crazy, Ernesto —"

"Do not let pride cost you your life!" He raises the gun. "The moment you appeared in front of me just now, I thought: this is it, I have waited too long, they have come for me. I should have run this morning. I will not make that mistake again. But first tell me exactly where they are." He waves the revolver at Leonard and takes a step forward.

"We're in a greenhouse, Ernesto. You can't just —"

"It doesn't matter. No one can see us from the hotel. With this rain no one can hear us. But it will not come to that. You will answer my question."

"Then I can go?"

"Then *I* can go."

A drop of rain falls through a crack in the glass roof and lands on the hand holding the revolver. Ernesto flinches and it jerks to one side.

"Okay, okay," says Leonard, raising his hands higher. "I'll be straight with you. Just lower the gun. You want to know where they are? There's two guys in a delivery van at the end of the driveway and a couple in their early sixties in the hotel pretending to be —"

"Don't lie to me!" shouts Ernesto, advancing on Leonard. The revolver is now pointing directly at his head.

"I have no idea where the team is! You think they sit in the same place all day like statues? They're always on the move. One thing you can be sure of is that they'll have watched us coming in here. This rain might mean they can't see us through the glass, but the flip side is that you won't be able to see *them*. You should run now, while you have the chance. Give yourself a head start – you're going to need it."

"No one knows the woods around here better than I do."

"What I don't understand is why you're going to such crazy lengths to escape. For someone in your position this will be painless – you must know that. Look at what happened to the illegals in the USA. One year from now you'll get swapped at Vienna airport for someone the Russians have caught and find yourself back home in Moscow."

"That's what I'm afraid of."

"What?"

"I'm not going to ask you again."

"I told you, I don't —"

Another drop of rain falls through the crack onto Ernesto's outstretched hand. He flinches again and this time he pulls the trigger. The glass above Leonard's head shatters all around him. Rain pours into the greenhouse.

"What are you doing?" shouts Leonard. "Put that thing down!" A piece of glass has cut the top of his head. He wipes blood from his eyes with the sleeve of his jacket. "This is madness, Ernesto. You don't need to run. Are you worried about what you did to Willa, is that what this is about? There's no evidence linking you to her, there's no murder charge waiting for you. I'm telling you, you'll be packed off home to a hero's welcome before you know it."

"Murder charge? What are you talking about?"

"Not even that. *Attempted* murder. But no one cares about that, Ernesto. Willa knew what she was doing when she signed up. She knew the risks. It won't get in the way of a swap. You'll be allowed to go home. But this" – he gestures towards the revolver – "this is completely different. This will put you in prison for the rest of your life. Even if you get through the surveillance cordon, you won't last on the run. Your picture's at every airport, every ferry terminal, every bus —"

"What are you talking about?"

"Just hand yourself in, it'll be —"

"No, about Willa!"

"What?"

"What did you say about Willa?" shouts Ernesto, stepping forward again.

"What do you mean?"

"What has happened to Willa?"

"Why are you asking *me*?" says Leonard.

"Damn you, what has happened to Willa?"

"How do you not know?"

Ernesto presses the revolver against Leonard's forehead.

"She's been in a coma for the last six weeks," says Leonard quickly. "Ever since you poisoned her."

Ernesto lets out a cry, steps back and drops the gun to the floor.

2

Ernesto looks as though he might faint. Leonard kicks the revolver into the far corner of the greenhouse. He sweeps a tray of small plastic pots off an old wicker chair and tries to help Ernesto onto it, but the gardener pushes Leonard away and drops to his knees.

For a full minute he does nothing except right the pots and repack them with spilled soil. "Poisoned?" he says finally. "Will she survive?"

"Are you really trying to tell me —"

"Will she survive?" says Ernesto.

"They haven't been able to identify the poison, which makes treatment difficult. What can you tell me about it?"

"What? I don't know what the poison is!"

"It'll make a huge difference to her chances if you tell me how it was delivered," says Leonard. "Was it food or drink? Perfume?"

"I don't know, I don't know."

"An injection?"

"How would I know?"

"Did you handle it at any stage?"

"It wasn't me, I swear it."

"Where is the poison now?"

Ernesto looks close to tears. With trembling hands he places the pots back in their tray and sweeps up what is left of the soil. At the far end of the greenhouse rain pours through the single broken pane like something from a child's drawing.

"We know Moscow wanted to kill her," says Leonard. "We've identified you, her handler, and we've identified the person they sent here with the poison. We've even heard two senior officers celebrating the fact they'd chopped down an English oak."

"What do you mean?"

"Willa is the English oak. They wanted to kill her —"

"The English oak is me, you imbecile! Because I am a gardener – what does Willa have to do with an oak tree? They were trying to kill me! They were trying to kill me! But somehow…"

"Why would they want to kill you?"

Ernesto puts his hands to his face and groans. "I know what happened," he says. "A guest left a bottle of weed-killer in one of the hotel rooms and the receptionist gave it to me. They thought I would use it. But instead I gave it to Willa for her geraniums. This must have been the poison. The guest … the guest must have been one of their… Oh God – what have I done? Can you tell her doctors? Will this help them treat her?"

"Why would Moscow want to kill you?" asks Leonard.

"Because this is what they do to traitors. However long it takes, however many years pass, they never forget – if you are one of their own and you turn your back on them, you will spend the rest of your days on the run. They will never stop looking for you."

"But why?" asks Leonard again. "What have you done to deserve that?"

Ernesto climbs off the floor and sits in the wicker chair with the tray of plants on his lap. He is still wearing his long green coat and the wide-brimmed straw hat. "Can I see her?" he asks.

"What's going on?"

"Can I see her?"

"As far as we're concerned, Ernesto, you're the one who tried to kill her. Can you persuade me otherwise?"

Ernesto is quiet for several minutes. Then he takes off his straw hat and begins to talk.

3

"I arrived here in 1985, young and enthusiastic, fresh out of training and ready to take control of the most promising British agent we had recruited in decades. A young Englishwoman had walked into the Russian embassy in The Hague, claimed that she worked for MI5 and explained that she wished to do harm to her employers. She was very angry about something but would not give any details. She was interviewed at length and instructed to return to London and await contact from her new handler, who would approach her on the street one day to ask the question 'Can you recommend a local teahouse which serves scones?' Exactly three weeks later I walked off the aeroplane with a set of impeccable documents in the pocket of my new suit. The real Ernesto had been a baby who contracted measles in a Brazilian favela at the age of seven months and died. The false Ernesto got to work immediately: he rented a room, he found work, he made contact with his agent.

"As you would expect, this was a very delicate stage in the development of an asset like Willa: she was frightened, guilty, excited, angry, remorseful – often all in the same meeting. My job was to calm her down and help her grow into an agent who would provide us with a treasure chest of secrets from the heart of the British establishment. This is one way of putting it. The other way is to say that my job was to bring her totally under our control.

"Do you know Willa? I can tell you the answer to this: you don't know her. You have met her, you have spoken to her at length. But this is the face she chose to present to her colleagues. This is nothing like her real face. This is nothing like the real Willa. Because the simple truth about her that I learned over the course of my first year in England was this: you cannot control a woman like Willa. You cannot tell her what to do.

"Nonetheless, I had my orders. I presented her with a list of information we wished to obtain. It was very simple: a staff list, telephone extensions, a list of properties used in London. Most of this we knew already, but this is how it works at the beginning. Small steps, so as not to alarm her – and of course we wanted to check she was being truthful. But you cannot imagine how difficult she was. She wanted a justification for every request. Who was it for? Why did they need it? What would they do with it? Would anyone be harmed? She disputed every answer I gave her, she questioned my judgement, she thought the tradecraft I used was substandard. She even mocked the clothes I wore to blend in among the English.

"Still I persevered. Expectations in Moscow were extremely high and the pressure on me was enormous, despite the fact that I was many hundreds of miles away from my superiors. I was determined to succeed. My reputation, my livelihood, my professional pride depended on it. My father was a highly decorated SVR officer, and his father was a member of the Cheka under the great Felix Dzerzhinsky. I had promised myself I would equal their achievements with those of my own, which would be even more remarkable for the fact that they would be fought for and won deep behind enemy lines. The illegals programme is the jewel in the crown of the Russian special services, and I was the illegal entrusted with the most precious agent of all. The president himself knew of my existence. I was determined that when he thought of me and the work I was doing his chest would swell with pride in the Soviet people and their battle to assume their rightful place on the world stage.

"So I used every trick and technique I had been taught, and a few more I made up. One month I pressed money on her to make it clear she needed to provide something significant in return for such handsome payments; the next month I refused to give her a penny. I told her I would be recalled to Moscow and shot if things did not change. I told her we could not justify such a level of risk and resources for an agent who was unproductive. I bought her expensive jewellery and tried to make her fall in love with me. I wrote a letter that I said was from the Russian president promising her a long and happy retirement in her very own dacha outside St Petersburg, and I showed her a picture I had cut from a magazine of a little cottage amid a snowy landscape, with smoke curling up from its chimney. I threatened to tell the British authorities about her so she would spend the rest of her days in prison. Oh, how she laughed at that one!

"As an agent she was not completely unproductive. What did she bring me during this first year? There were a few things, especially during those periods when she was most angry with your office. The names of some senior officers, the ones she disliked most. We learned from her how the vetting process works, but this was something we knew already as we had instructed many agents over the years to apply for a job. There were a few pieces of soft intelligence about office culture, the subjects people complain about, which room on which floor is used by which department.

"But it was not enough to satisfy my superiors, especially as the months passed. They would write to me: 'Congratulations on your recent report. There continues to be much interest here in your project. But we need more. You must push harder. Consider meeting your friend more often to increase the productivity of the relationship.' It was straightforward to meet in those days – before mobile phones, before cameras on every street. We had agreed that Willa would pretend to have an interest in cathedrals, and so on the last Friday of every month we would meet in a different town. Canterbury, Ely, St Albans, Salisbury, Winchester – we travelled everywhere. The plan was always the same. Stand in the middle of the cathedral transept at midday. If you believe it is safe to proceed with the meeting, hold a local map in your left hand. If you suspect you have been followed, or if you have by chance bumped into someone you know, hold the map in your right hand. Assuming I had also not observed any surveillance, I would then walk directly past her to a dark, quiet corner of the cathedral, at which point she would approach me to ask the time. From there we would proceed to the coffee shop – I used to choose cathedrals with a coffee shop in the crypt – and begin our discussions.

"It pleased me greatly to be doing it this way. I had the idea that while eating scones and sipping tea we were in fact planting a bomb in each of these cities, that together we would work our way around the country like sappers and at a moment of our choosing press the button and bring the whole rotten British establishment crashing to the ground. The only thing that spoiled this vision was Willa herself.

"So I made a new plan. The problem, I decided, was that we did not know each other well enough. She needed to feel a personal connection to her handler in order to trust him and fulfil her potential as an agent. With the reluctant agreement of my superiors, I put to one side all matters of intelligence, all requests, all demands for greater productivity. I stopped trying to exert any control over her. I even stopped paying her money. We followed the same tradecraft procedures, but apart from that we might have been two old friends meeting for a reunion. We talked about the films we had seen, the books we had read, the museum exhibitions we had enjoyed. I taught her about Russian literature – about Pushkin, about Pasternak. She fixed my broken English. She encouraged me to read the modern English poets. From there our conversation moved to personal subjects: childhood experiences, our parents, first loves. Of course, at first I was guarded, as is every handler with their agent. I did not want to provide her with personal information that might allow her employers to learn my real identity if we were discovered and she was interrogated. I changed certain details, I even borrowed stories I had heard from friends and passed them off as my own. But it is impossible to construct a false life that can withstand genuine, alert, sympathetic curiosity. There is a warmth in the air generated by someone leaning towards you with a smile, with eyes that stay fixed on you, with a heart generous enough to accept all your awkwardness and guilt and shame. And this warmth, over a period of six months, was more than sufficient to melt the mask I was using. I told you that my purpose in adopting this new approach with her was to change minds. Well, it worked. But it turned out that the person who changed their mind was me. One day I simply looked across the table at her and realized what had happened: I was no longer her handler and she was no longer my agent. Over the course of six months we had talked our way out of that artificial and unbalanced relationship and into something different. We were friends. More than that, we were best friends. It was a conversion, you might say – an underground conversion, and beneath a cathedral of all places. Could anything be more appropriate?"

He looks at the plant pots on his lap. With a careful thumb he brushes soil from each tiny leaf.

"When does a story end?" he says, more to himself than to Leonard. "Over the following months my reports back to Moscow became less frequent and eventually stopped. Several times I prepared a message telling them that I was no longer able to continue in my role, but I could not find the right words for this, and I knew they would not understand. This is not a job you can simply retire from. They would think I was defecting, that British intelligence had turned me. I even considered returning to Moscow to show them I was under no one's control and to resign formally.

"Eventually someone from the embassy used the emergency protocol to make direct contact with me. They must have been desperate to take such a risk because of the possibility that as a diplomat he was under surveillance. I had moved house by this time, but somehow they found out where I was living. When I came home one afternoon a piece of red chewing gum had been stuck to the handle of my door. I knew I was being observed and that someone would be waiting for me in the bandstand in Battersea Park in exactly one hour. I went there and saw him from far away holding an ice cream. I can spot a Russian official in a crowd at a hundred yards. I approached him and explained that my circumstances had changed, that I bore him and the country he represented no ill will, that I would carry my professional secrets to the grave but that he should consider my employment to have come to an end. He did not try to argue with me.

What of the asset, he asked. The asset has changed her mind, I told him. The asset does not wish to have any further contact with you. Her mind is also made up. Then I walked away. It is hard to believe now, but I thought that might be the end of it. Two years later they tried to kill me. The first time was a man with a knife in Hyde Park. Five years later someone tried to push me in front of a train. In total there were six attempts over twenty years. It only stopped when Willa came to me one day with an advertisement she had found for a gardener in a country hotel. But now they have found me here. And I gave the poison intended for me to the person who means most to me in the world."

4

The wind has dropped outside. Rain splashes into puddles on the cold greenhouse floor.

"Were you in love with her?" asks Leonard.

"Why are you using the past tense?" Ernesto has recovered his equilibrium. Decades on the run have bred in him a resilience that quickly reasserts itself.

"Are you in love with her?" asks Leonard.

"There is nothing romantic between us, if this is what you mean. Do I love her? If you do not know the answer to this question, you have not been listening."

"You said Willa had one face for the office and another face for her real life," says Leonard. "Why?"

"Have you *really* not been listening?"

"I've been listening to a frankly unbelievable story about someone who flirted with betrayal, handed over a few completely unimportant secrets, but for the past, what, the past twenty-five years, has been a model citizen."

"It is your choice whether to believe this or not."

"Her betrayal stops but she continues to lie to everyone around her. Does that make sense to you?"

Ernesto shrugs. "Maybe she fell into this habit in the early years."

"Why not change it? Once she had reset the relationship with you, once it was just a question of friendship, why maintain this exhausting facade? She might think: I'm twenty-five years clear of a moment of youthful madness and absolutely nothing has happened in that time. No suspicious questions, no accusations. I can relax now. I can afford to drop this low profile, have a drink with colleagues once in a while, maybe even accumulate some personal possessions."

"If anyone had discovered her friendship with me, she would have been forced to leave her job. She was visiting me whenever we could find the opportunity. And I just told you that in these twenty years there were six attempts on my life. We both had to be very careful. It was how we lived."

"But why did she stay in the job all these years? If she was angry enough at the office to walk into a Russian embassy and volunteer her services, why didn't she just leave once she'd decided not to be an agent? It makes no sense that she would stay."

Ernesto shrugs again.

"What's the answer?" says Leonard.

"She had her reasons."

"What were they?"

"It's not for me to say."

"That's not good enough."

"It's nothing that did any harm," says Ernesto. "On the contrary. She wanted to make a contribution."

"A significant part of the case against her is to do with her conduct as a vetting officer," says Leonard. "There was something unusual —"

"You're going to tell me she had an idiosyncratic approach to her job."

"More than that."

"It was nothing to do with me, Leonard. I never asked her to let this person in or prevent that person from joining – neither did my former employers. They probably would have done so if the relationship had progressed. But Willa was entirely independent. She had her own reasons for everything she did."

"Which were?"

"She had a … project. A passion. Let us call it that."

"She deliberately let in candidates she believed would undermine the stability of the organization."

"Undermine the stability of the organization?" says Ernesto. "I am disappointed to hear such language from you. Who is the Russian here? This is something my former colleagues would say. Tell me this, what does it mean to be stable in a world that is changing all the time? Look at the trees all around us. We can learn a lot from them. Their stability comes from their roots, which are constantly growing."

"It's certainly the most poetic defence of betrayal I've ever heard," says Leonard. "The fault lies with British intelligence and its unwillingness to simply bend to Russian attempts to steal its secrets. We should be opening the windows to a wind from the east that will gently carry our secrets out of the window and onto the —"

"Don't be an idiot. Willa loves your office – she loves its history, its mission, astonishingly even some of the people. She grew up at the knee of relatives with experience of Europe in the first half of this century. She is no naive ideologue. She accepts that the stability this country has enjoyed for so long comes at a price. It is just that like any sensible person she wants to keep that price down. She is not a traitor – she just drives a hard bargain." Ernesto slumps in the chair. All the air has gone out of him. "We had our plans – our retirement plans, you might call them," he says. "Willa was going to sell her flat in London, and I have saved a little money over the years. Last time she was here we agreed to buy a cottage on one of the Scottish islands, as far away and well hidden from Russian assassins as we could possibly be. To reach it you would have to cross the water by rowing boat. We would tell people we were brother and sister. Willa would say she had a violent ex-husband and ask local people to tell us if any strangers came to town. We would have dogs – lots of dogs. And chickens, some rabbits, maybe even a goat. I would build a garden to grow all the food we needed. Willa would write poems and paint pictures while I worked outside, and in the evenings we would sit together and look at the sea and tell each other stories."

Leonard and Ernesto are both quiet. The rain on the glass above them has its own voice: low, intimate, musical. It says things incredibly familiar and deeply strange.

It is Ernesto who finally speaks. "What will happen?" he asks.

"No one will believe your story," says Leonard. "I'm not sure I believe it myself. Even if you were telling the truth, even if you wanted to cooperate, your secrets are decades old. The office will want to keep this very quiet. It'd be humiliating to admit there's been an illegal living here for thirty years. I imagine you'll be put on ice and quietly swapped the next time Moscow catches a British spy."

"This is a death sentence." Ernesto stands and places the tray of plants on the trestle table. In one smooth motion he swings the rucksack onto his back. "Come on," he says. "Let's go."

"One more question," asks Leonard.

"With you there's always one more question."

"How do you know my name?"

"What?" asks Ernesto.

"You used my real name. You called me Leonard. How do you know my name?"

Ernesto puts the straw hat back on his head, ties the string in a knot under his chin and smiles. "How do you think?" he says.

FROM THE ARCHIVES

6A

Daily Press Summary
11 March 1993

Islington Gazette
Brush with Death at Angel
By Samantha Lewes

Rush hour commuters were startled yesterday to witness the near death of a man beneath a train at Angel Underground station.

Sophie, 34, a secretary from Croydon, said that she had been standing a few feet away when she saw a man stumble at the edge of the platform just before a train passed through the station at speed.

"At first I thought it was an accident," she told the *Gazette*. "But then he steadied himself and I saw this other man shove him really hard in the back. He would have fallen right in front of the train if one of the other passengers hadn't grabbed hold of his arm at the last minute."

British Transport Police said they were examining camera footage but had been unable to locate either the alleged assailant or his victim, both of whom fled the station before police arrived on the scene.

NOT PROTECTIVELY MARKED

6B

CONFIDENTIAL

FROM: Heathrow Airport Special Branch
TO: MI5 (Russia Leads)
DATE: 22 October 2004
SUBJECT: Russian national briefly detained

1. Officers at Heathrow stopped a Russian national named Makhmud AHMADOV attempting to board a flight to Moscow this afternoon.

2. AHMADOV was first observed by officers in the duty-free area with an apparent wound to his abdomen that had bled through his shirt. He had fresh bruising around his left eye and the knuckles of both hands were swollen.

3. Speaking through a police interpreter, AHMADOV initially refused medical attention, but reluctantly agreed when told that he would not be allowed to board a flight in his condition. Upon removal of his shirt for treatment, officers observed that his entire torso was covered with tattoos, including skulls, tigers, a spider and manacles around the wrists. According to the interpreter, the nature of the

tattoos indicated that AHMADOV had spent a period of time in a Russian prison, although AHMADOV himself denied this. The interpreter also speculated that based on his name and accent AHMADOV was likely to be of Chechen origin.

4. The duty doctor dressed a number of shallow lacerations across AHMADOV's stomach and assessed that there were no medical grounds to prevent him boarding a plane.

5. Officers searched AHMADOV's hand luggage and found a substantial amount of medical-grade painkillers and £1,270 in cash. He refused to explain the source of the money and became verbally aggressive when informed that officers intended to seize the painkillers.

6. As we had no reason to detain AHMADOV further and could find no adverse intelligence trace against his name or passport number, we allowed him to board an Aeroflot flight to Moscow this evening. We have added his details to the Home Office database and would recommend that any future applications for a visa are denied.

CONFIDENTIAL

6C

T9 (Serious and Organized Crime)

SUBJECT: Voicemail message left by Kevin MCDOUGAL
DATE: 13 February 2006

1.   Transcriber's note: Please add to file. MCDOUGAL tried
      to call "Cuntface" (possibly George BELLEVUE) 4 times
      before leaving the message below. His tone throughout
      is irate. The "flats" he refers to are the 16 properties he
      owns in the King's Cross area.

BEGINS

1436: Pick up, cuntface. This is last chance saloon for you.
You're supposed to be looking after my properties, you fucking
nitwit. Sharon was showing someone one of the flats this morning and what did she find? The door to 14c has been smashed
in. There's a fucking noose round the shower pipe. A noose!
I'd like to put it round your neck. Not to mention blood all

over the bathroom. Sharon burst into tears when she got back to the office. Very upsetting for a young lady to see things like that. She's been a fucking nightmare ever since. Tenant was a shifty little bald runt from Brazil. Please please please tell me you got the full deposit from him. He had so many plants in there it was like a fucking rainforest and now soil's trampled into the carpet. It'll have to be changed. If you didn't get a deposit it's coming out of your pay packet. Call me.

ENDS

TOP SECRET

CHAPTER SEVEN

Thursday, 2014

Leonard is walking to the station in the rain when his phone rings.

"What happened in the greenhouse?"

"Franny, I don't think —"

"Are you all right? That cut on your head… What happened, Leonard?"

"I don't know exactly. It took me by surprise. I can imagine it took everyone by surprise."

"Are you all right?"

He touches the cut. "I'll be okay."

"Are you alone?"

"Yes."

"So … what happened?" she asks. "I'm on tenterhooks. We all are."

"We should probably discuss this when I'm back in the office. Was the audio quality all right, though? Could you hear us?"

"We didn't hear anything."

He stops. "What did you say?"

"We didn't hear a single word," says Franny.

"I thought every square foot of the hotel and grounds was covered by cameras and microphones."

"I thought so too. Turns out it's just too big. Across the whole property there's half a dozen or more sheds, outhouses, cellars, storerooms… There's a concrete bunker somewhere. He's even got a workshop filled with circuit boards and soldering irons and all sorts of electrical bits and pieces. They've put a microphone in there because most days he spends an hour or more tinkering, but he's never spent much time in the greenhouse so they searched it but didn't install any kit. You said he took you by surprise, Leonard. In what way?"

"Wait, wait. Let me get this straight. Are you telling me you didn't hear *anything*?"

"They saw you approach him, and when the two of you walked off in the direction of the greenhouse they tried to cover you from a distance. But it was impossible to see anything through the rain. Jesus, Leonard. Why are you being so weird? What happened? Why were you in there for so long?"

A few hours earlier he was listening to Remnant explaining that he had tried to engineer this precise situation, a private conversation between Leonard and the illegal, as a way of testing Leonard's loyalty. It is therefore almost certainly untrue, he thinks, that they didn't have a microphone in the greenhouse. They are trying to salvage what they can from the wreckage of their operation. Once again they are trying to test him.

"Leonard?"

Why does he hesitate? This is his chance to prove his loyalty. He should tell them everything.

"Leonard, are you still there?"

The future is already written, this is what he believes. He tries to discern its outline through the rain. Water soaks through his shoes. What does he see? He sees a meeting room with no windows, a meeting room packed with over a hundred years of experience. He sees curiosity hardening into certainty that this story of friendship in cathedral crypts is simply too ridiculous to swallow.

"Shall I send a car for you? Are you all right?"

He sees the pine table, he sees the carpet squares.

An analyst points out that very little in Ernesto's story can be independently verified. In fact, she says, it feels as though this story has been deliberately put together in a way to obviate the need for Ernesto to provide any intelligence of value to establish his bona fides.

"Can you tell me where you are?"

He sees three clocks on the wall, he sees a locked door.

A lawyer suggests that if a short-term solution is required, Ernesto could be arrested for discharging a firearm. A resettlement officer tells the assembled group that accepting Ernesto's story at face value and allowing him to stay in the UK will come with a responsibility to protect him for the rest of his life, which will be prohibitively expensive. An old Russia hand in the corner stirs briefly to reflect aloud that illegals go through an extremely rigorous selection process to ensure they are robust enough to withstand much greater inducements than mere friendship. Someone with no experience of anything suggests a polygraph.

"Wait where you are. I'm sending a car."

Remnant bangs the table to bring the meeting to a close. He demands that the illegal who has been operating under their noses for three decades and making them all look like bloody fools is arrested this minute for the attempted murder of a British citizen and left to languish in prison until some fool in Whitehall decides he should be swapped for some fool in Moscow.

Leonard starts walking again. He surprises himself by saying, "He wanted to give me a cutting."

"He cut you?" says Franny. "With a knife? Is that what happened to your head?"

"No, he gave me a *tree* cutting."

"What?" says Franny. "What? He gave you *what*?"

"The first time I spoke to him we talked about one of the trees. He remembered the conversation and offered me a cutting. It would have been odd to refuse, so I went with him."

"Hang on. A *tree* cutting? He offered you a *tree* cutting? But you were in the greenhouse for ages."

"He was talkative," says Leonard. "He wanted to explain how to look after it, what kind of compost to use, how much water it'll need. I didn't think I could just walk out. And it was raining so heavily. I suspect I was an excuse to stay dry."

"When the team moved in they saw that one of the glass panels in the roof was smashed. They said it hadn't been broken before."

"He knocked it loose with a broom handle when —"

"What?"

"There was a leak – it had damaged a few of the plants in there – and he was trying to nudge the glass pane back into position with a broom handle. But he pushed too hard and it came crashing down."

"You can't imagine how close they came to going in, Leonard. At one point Remnant made the call and then immediately changed his mind. One of the team was literally touching the door handle. You know that camouflage rucksack he had with him? They'd never seen it before today – he went into the woods this afternoon and came out holding it a few minutes later as though it was something he'd hidden in case of emergency. Since then Remnant's had half a dozen people crawling through the undergrowth looking for a cache of some sort. Everyone's on high alert. When you didn't come out for ages they started to imagine the worst. Someone even suggested he might have a weapon. They sent one of the team to crawl right up to the glass and peer through, but all he could see was your friend sitting on a chair with a tray of plant pots balanced on his knees."

"What's he doing now?" Leonard asks.

"In an armchair in his cottage staring into space. Remnant's worst nightmare is that he bolts via some route he's prepared. He might have a vehicle somewhere, a set of false documents, even a disguise. Then it's a needle in a haystack. There's a million and one ways off this island. It's also possible the Russian embassy in London will get involved, that they've got a plan to hide him in diplomatic cargo. But at the same time he might not have realized all this is going on around him. He might try to make contact with other agents he's running, which would be incredibly useful. There's an opportunity here to roll up his entire network. It's a balancing act: the cordon has to be close but not too close. Remnant's starting to crack up under the pressure. He's pacing back and forth in the ops room shouting at anyone who catches his eye. Did you manage to reassure our friend that there's not going to be an immigration raid any time soon?"

"I think so. I'm not sure he even remembered it. Can I ask you something, Franny?" he says. "You've looked at him more closely than anyone. Since arriving in this country all those years ago, has he ever left for a trip, even a short one, to another country?"

"Not that we know of."

"It's odd, don't you think? In every other case I've worked on, the Russians have always found a way to spirit their man back home for a few days to check they're still onside, give them a pep talk, make sure they're focused on the right things. At the very least you'd expect him to have had third-country meetings with his superiors. But he hasn't been anywhere."

"You're not doubting what he is, Leonard, are you?"

"I wonder if we've got it right."

"All it takes to win you over is a tree cutting. If only I'd known it was that easy. I've got a cactus on my desk you could have. The whole thing, too – not just a cutting."

Leonard is walking past a row of houses. Dark sodden clothes hang stiffly from a washing line like bats. He can't understand why no one has taken it in. It's hard to remember a time when it wasn't raining.

"Do you know what I think it is?" Franny is saying. "As *one* target of this operation, you're sympathetic to the *other* target. Is that possible? Remnant got it wrong about you, so he might have got it wrong about the other guy." Leonard hears someone speaking in the background. Franny lowers her voice. "I'm not supposed to tell you this," she says quickly, "but they were watching you in the London flat. They were watching as you pulled out the wires and smashed the walls. I think they've gone back to not trusting you again. I really shouldn't be telling you this." Someone calls her name. "I've got to go. Remnant wanted me to tell you in a casual and relaxed manner – those were his words – to pop back in for a friendly chat this evening. I just want you to be prepared for a few questions about your … state of mind. I don't know what he's planning. He's locked in a strategy meeting and will be for the next couple of hours at least. Willa's woken up from her coma and they're working out what to do with her. He won't get round to you for a little while yet. But get your story straight."

"Willa's awake?"

"Awake and lucid, they say."

Suddenly he sees it.

"Leonard? Are you there?"

He sees the outline of his future rushing towards him through the driving rain.

CHAPTER EIGHT

Thursday, 2230

1

Leonard clutches a bouquet of flowers to his chest and steps through the doors of the hospital ward. At this late hour the lights are dimmed. The only member of staff in sight is a cleaner mopping the floor. She sings a hymn to the irregular beep of machines talking to each other; it lends a jazzy syncopation to her singing that she probably doesn't intend. Leonard has to go all the way down the corridor to find someone who can help him, and it takes another few minutes for the ward manager to arrive. "I'm looking for Willa Karlsson," he explains.

"And you are?"

"Her nephew."

"I don't think we've been told she has any family," she says. "Besides, access to her room is restricted. Do you know what time it is?"

"I've just flown in to see her," says Leonard. He rummages through his bag for his alias passport and holds it out to her. In his experience people are much more impressed by things like passports than they should be.

"I've been in touch with the government – in fact, there was a message from them when I landed, saying she's woken up. Is that right? Is she awake?"

The ward manager isn't sure what to do with his passport but reluctantly takes it. She examines his picture. "Who have you been in contact with at the Home Office, Mr Karlsson?" she asks. She can't resist the urge to flick through the rest of the pages, having seen it done a hundred times or more by professionals as she passed through airports, although she has no way of judging whether any of the stamps are real or were added a few days earlier in case something like this arose.

"Charles something," he says. "Charles Remnant? Is that right?"

She glares at him; he wonders whether Remnant has used a different name with her. She continues to examine the passport. He can see she is beginning to enjoy this new authority bestowed upon her as gatekeeper to a twilight kingdom where machines do the important work and humans mop the floor. "Mr Remnant is on his way in at this very moment," she says, squinting to read the small text above an exit stamp. "If you take a seat you won't have long to wait."

"He told me to meet him here. Can I sit with Willa until he arrives? I hate the idea of her waking up without a familiar face by her bedside."

"He won't be long," she says. "There's a coffee machine downstairs and a snack machine along the corridor."

"That's very kind. I haven't slept much in the last few days so some coffee would be very welcome. I don't know if you've spoken to Mr Remnant, but he strikes me from our phone calls as being quite … businesslike. What you'd expect – what you'd *want* – from someone in his position. But it'd be lovely to sit with my aunt for just ten minutes before that and hold her hand. I know Mr Remnant will have a million and one questions about what happened, and it might relax her if I have a chance to see her first."

She holds out his passport. As though freeing a hand to take it from her, he fumbles the bouquet and drops it to the floor.

"Those million and one questions are extremely important for her treatment," she says, waggling the passport at him. "She might have woken up, but she's most certainly not out of the woods."

Leonard doesn't want to take the passport from her – he doesn't want this role play to end. As a ward manager she has expertise and authority but as a border guard she has no idea what to do next, no idea what exactly she can and can't demand of this weary and emotional traveller on his knees in front of her. "Absolutely," he says, standing up with the flowers sprayed across his chest. "The priority is her treatment. The whole family is agreed on that. And I know you're doing the most incredible job looking after her. When Mr Remnant arrives I'll let him get on with asking those important questions." He adjusts the flowers. "To be honest, I was just planning to show her some baby pictures on my phone. My brother's had a little girl and he's chosen Willa as her middle name. You wouldn't believe how many pictures I've got, there's upwards of —"

"All right, all right." She's had enough of this. "I'll have one of the nurses sit with you in her room until Mr Remnant arrives." She steps aside to grant him entry. "You can collect your passport on the way out."

2

The only light comes from a silent television at the end of an extendable arm several feet from Willa's face. The rest of the room is so dark Leonard can barely make out its edges and corners. Machines hunker in the gloom like brooding country relatives impatient for their inheritance. The nurse finds a chair and places it several feet away from Willa. It would be impossible to get any closer. Her bed is surrounded by stiff, clear, protective sheeting that hangs from the ceiling to the floor.

"Make yourself at home," says the nurse. Her voice bruises the silence.

Leonard allows himself to look at Willa properly for the first time. It is hard to discern the outline of a body beneath the bed sheets. Papery hands are folded over her chest, and dandelion-white hair sprays thinly outwards across the pillow from a face that is almost unrecognizable. Leonard reaches for the back of a chair to steady himself. The poison has gouged pockmarks from burned, yellow skin that is draped loosely like a dust sheet over cheekbones, a brow, her chin. She has lost so much weight her head itself seems shrunk, except for her eyes, which are large and unblinking and don't move from the television.

"Willa?" says Leonard. "It's me, it's your nephew." In the presence of her suffering his professional games seem enormously trivial. "They've said I can sit with you for a few minutes before the man from the government comes."

He wonders how to explain anything with the nurse in the room.

"Can she hear me?" he asks.

"Oh yes. She's quite lucid, and she has bursts of energy. But you should expect her to tire quickly."

"I brought some flowers from your friend's garden, Willa, but I've been told to leave them outside."

He touches the plastic sheeting that surrounds her bed. It glistens like slime across a whale's gaping mouth, as though Willa has been scooped whole from the watery darkness of the night.

"Is this necessary?"

"Just a precaution," says the nurse. "There's very little risk to others at this point. Whatever the poison was, it's done its damage and disappeared."

In the corridor outside the cleaner starts another hymn. "Dear Lord and Father of mankind," she sings, "forgive our foolish ways."

"Willa?" Leonard says, leaning in. "There's lots to tell you."

Willa extends a thin hand to pick up a plastic cup from the tray beside her, and when she lifts her head to take a sip, strands of white hair remain on the pillow. She tries to replace the cup but misses the tray by a few inches and the cup falls to the floor. Leonard stands up.

"Never mind," says the nurse. "Let me fill that up for you with some fresh water."

"No," says Willa.

They both turn to look at her.

"Hot tea," she says slowly. "Milk and two sugars. And a biscuit. Not one of those cheap ones from the nurses' station. A bourbon, or at the very least a chocolate digestive."

"Look who's come back to life," says the nurse with a smile as she bustles out of the door.

3

Leonard pulls the plastic sheeting to one side. He drags his chair closer to the bed. "We haven't got much time," he says.

"Your bedside manner could do with some work, young man."

"Before Remnant gets here, I mean."

She expends an enormous amount of energy trying to pull herself upright.

"Willa, they know about Ernesto."

"You seem to have your pronouns in a muddle."

"What do you mean?" he asks.

"If Charles Remnant is the man from the government, as you described him, then who exactly are you?"

"My name is Leonard, I'm —"

"I know what your *name* is, Leonard. Do you think anyone else dresses like that? Do you think I thought you were my nephew? What I mean is, *why* are *you* here?"

There is a force emanating from her that he has never seen before. How did she keep it under control, and for all those years? How did she not blind everyone?

"I need to know about Ernesto, Willa," he says. "I need to hear it from you."

"This is to be one of your famous interrogations, is it?" She coughs. "Bear in mind I've asked the nurse for a cup of tea and a biscuit, not a three-course dinner."

"I've spoken to him."

"Is he all right? With this hot weather he'll doubtless be fussing no end about his garden."

"He's in a very tight spot, I won't lie to you."

"Oh?"

"Remnant has him surrounded."

She considers Leonard carefully. "That's quite a disclosure," she says. "Does Remnant know you're discussing his operational tactics with me?"

"Not exactly." He pulls his chair closer. "Willa, why did you volunteer to the Russians all those years ago?"

She looks away.

"What happened? What was the trigger?"

She sighs.

"How long did it go on for?"

She raises a hand dismissively.

"I've heard a version, a very partial version, from Ernesto, Willa. That you approached them more than thirty years ago but quickly changed your mind. That Ernesto was your handler but doesn't work for them any more. That they were trying to kill him, not you. No one is going to believe it. Can you do any better?"

"I thought we were short of time. But here you are, wanting me to tell you a story you don't even believe all over again. Is there really nothing better you can think of to ask?"

"Is he a threat?"

"Ernesto? To whom, for goodness' sake?"

"This country," says Leonard.

"Is Ernesto a threat to this country? Leonard, dear. I'll forgive you such simplistic language only because you're clearly under pressure. He's a threat to roses, I'll tell you that, the way he chops them back with no sense of aesthetics or proportion. He's a threat to the hares that steal his runner beans and the birds that eat his seeds. He once caught a hedgehog by mistake in one of his squirrel traps and the poor thing limped for at least a week afterwards. I told him, it's a good thing you're not trying to pass yourself off as an Englishman, given the way you keep a garden. Not a straight line in sight. There's only a lawn because the owner threatened to sack him if he didn't put one in. They fought a pitched battle over every square foot of the thing. Do you think they'll allow him to stay?"

"No."

"What will they do?"

"Put him through the wringer."

"I thought as much," says Willa. "It's Remnant's favourite instrument after all, the wringer. I imagine he has a workshop somewhere full of them, one for every occasion."

"Once they've finished they'll send him home."

"Home? I'm not sure that's quite the right word for a basement where they shoot you in the back of the head." Her eyes fill with tears. "It's been nice to see you, Leonard. I mean that. You were one of my favourites. But do you think you could leave me alone? I need to prepare myself for Charles Remnant. Like a bride on her wedding night. Now there's an idea – if I can't talk him into letting Ernesto stay, maybe I should flirt with him." She smoothes her hair into place and pouts. "How do I look?"

Leonard doesn't know how to answer.

"I'm teasing you," she says. "Always so serious, Leonard. They won't give me a mirror, but I can see enough of my reflection in the television screen to know what's happening. I know my body – it's already starting to shut down. They put the poison in a bottle of weedkiller, did you know that? Remnant must have chuckled at that detail. No doubt he sees me as a weed to be pulled from his neat English lawn and tossed onto the compost heap."

"Why didn't you call someone?" Leonard asks. "Why did you hide the bottle? It would have helped the doctors no end if they'd been able to identify the poison."

"Thank you for reminding me. It would be extremely kind if you could let the relevant people know that the bottle is somewhere on the roof of my building, wrapped in as much silver foil as I could find in my kitchen. There's no way up there, but it's been bothering me no end that someone might stumble upon it by accident one day and fall ill. I had a good half hour, you know. As soon as I touched the bottle, I knew – I could feel on my fingertips that something wasn't right. What would you do if you knew you had half an hour left, Leonard? Once I'd got rid of the bottle, I sat and looked out of my window and tried to feel grateful for everything I've had in my life. I thought about my parents, I thought about painting, I thought about my job. And, oh, I thought about Ernesto. I thought a lot about Ernesto."

"A bottle of poison next to your body would have immediately confirmed Russian involvement," he says. "That's why you threw it onto the roof. You were protecting Ernesto."

"Leonard, as much as I'm enjoying this conversation, I really would appreciate a few minutes to get my thoughts in order before Charles Remnant arrives."

"Is it true then, what he said? Despite who he worked for, despite what he came here to do, despite your offer to work for them, is this all simply about friendship?"

"Oh, there's nothing *simple* about friendship, Leonard. There were plenty of times Ernesto would say something and I would think to myself, you might not be in the enemy camp, but you're certainly not clear of it either. You're in a tunnel somewhere underneath the perimeter fence. There were days I had to stop myself stamping on the ground above his head and shouting for the guards, 'He's here! Take him back! He's trying to escape!' *Simple* is not the word, Leonard. We all live in our own little prison camps, but there is a way to tunnel to each other, provided we're patient, provided we're willing to change direction, provided we can accept that the other person will sometimes want to stamp on the ground above our heads."

Someone starts talking in the corridor.

"You said you thought about your job," he says. "In what you believed was your last half hour. What did you think about it?"

"Oh, Leonard – give a tired old lady a rest, will you?"

"That's why Remnant suspects you, Willa. It's not just about Ernesto. It's because of your record, it's because of who you chose to let into the Service, even after you claim to have broken contact with the Russians. It wasn't accidental, was it? None of it was. You had a plan."

"I thought about my first day as a vetting officer. 'Keep out the bad apples,' they said."

The door swings open.

"Apples?" says the nurse, bustling in with a cup of tea. "What's this about apples? Have you changed your mind about the biscuits?"

"Certainly not," says Willa firmly.

The nurse places the cup on a table next to Willa's bed. "There are rumours of home-made shortbread in the next ward," says the nurse. "Let me go and investigate."

"The first clue in a vetting interview," says Willa once the door has closed, "is the candidate's choice of biscuit. You can see that the best ones have considered which kind of biscuit to offer their vetting officer, which biscuit screams patriotism."

"Willa —"

"Nothing ever *whispers* patriotism, that's for sure."

"Willa —"

"Shortbread, now that's a clever choice. Your typical vetting officer would warm to a candidate who offers shortbread. Shortbread says traditional, shortbread says —"

"Willa," says Leonard, "was I one of your bad apples?"

"You? A bad apple? Stop going on, Leonard, will you? It's my insides being eaten by a Russian worm, not yours. Drop me on the floor and I'll go —"

"He knew my name. Ernesto knew my name."

"Splat."

There are raised voices in the corridor.

"Willa, please tell me. We haven't got long. Did you have another motive in allowing me to join the office?"

"I've never liked that thing they call you. What is it again?"

"The rat-catcher. Willa, please —"

"Leonard, what are you asking me really? Do you expect me to tell you something about yourself that you don't already know?"

He starts to speak, but at that moment the nurse comes in with a plate of shortbread, and when he turns back to Willa she's staring at the television screen with a blank expression on her dying face.

4

"You've tired her out," says the nurse. "Shall we leave her alone for a bit? Before the man from the government comes? She'll need her energy for that."

"Any sign of him?" asks Leonard.

"Not yet."

He looks around for a reason to stay. "Maybe if I just sit here," he says. "I can —"

"Come along," says the nurse. "You've had a good chat."

"I'll read to her," he says. "She's always loved books."

"No you won't."

"Willa, I've got some of your books here with me." He reaches for his bag. He's been carrying her books around with him all week.

"That's quite enough from you," says the nurse.

Leonard doesn't have time to select a book so lifts out the first one his fingers touch. "*Bent double, like old beggars under sacks,*" he reads, letting the book fall open. "*Knock-kneed, coughing like hags, we cursed through sludge, Till on the haunting flares we turned our backs, And towards our distant rest began to trudge.*"

"Goodness gracious, is that supposed to relax her?" says the nurse. "Come on. It's high time —"

Leonard takes out another book. "*It is the individuals who have fewer ties and are much more uncertain and morally weaker upon whom spiritual progress depends in such communities; they are the men who make new and manifold experiments.*" He glances up to see if Willa is listening. "*Innumerable men of this sort perish because of their weakness without any very visible effect; but in general ... they loosen up and from time to time inflict a wound upon the stable element of a community. Precisely in this wounded and weakened spot the whole structure is inoculated, as it were, with something new.*"

"You'll put *me* into a coma if you read any more of that," says the nurse.

Leonard reaches for another book.

"If you're not going to budge," says the nurse, "try this instead." She hands him a magazine. "Celebrity news is always a safe bet. Page twelve. But —"

There are voices outside.

"I wager that's Mr Remnant," says the nurse. "Shall we have a look?" She opens the door and steps outside.

"Willa," says Leonard. "Why did you let me in?"

She turns to him. "Let's find out, shall we?" she says.

His decision surprises him with its speed, with its immovable heft, as though it didn't so much arrive as reveal that it had been there all along. He reaches for her hand. "Do you have a way of getting in touch with Ernesto?" he asks.

She smiles at him.

"I've heard about his workshop," he says. "I can't imagine what else he's been doing with circuit boards if it's not making some piece of equipment the two of you use." He takes a mobile phone from his bag, shows it to her and slips it beneath her pillow. "With a little help," he says, "do you think you could walk?"

FROM THE ARCHIVES

8A

8 June 1984

Dear Director,

In light of the delicacy of the matter at hand, we sent an experienced officer to conduct a follow-up vetting interview with Miss Willa Karlsson this week. You will recall that Miss Karlsson is an exceptional candidate in her late twenties who has performed to a high standard during every stage of the recruitment process. You will also recall that her first vetting officer registered some concern following an interview with one of her character referees. The latest report is copied below.

BEGINS

Miss Karlsson greeted me at the entrance to her modest family residence in South London and introduced me to her elderly parents, who left to take the dog for a walk around their local park.

My first impression of Miss Karlsson was that she is an intelligent, confident and friendly young woman with an appealing demeanour. She had seen my arrival by car and made a comment suggesting she had taken note of the folded newspaper on the dashboard, which demonstrates good observational skills. She was dressed in a clean white shirt, red cardigan and tweed skirt; the only jewellery on display was a pair of small gold stud earrings.

After we had taken our seats in the living room and Miss Karlsson had offered me a cup of coffee, she asked after her first vetting officer and the reason for this second interview. I explained that it was routine to interview candidates more than once if there were questions that needed to be resolved, and took the opportunity to emphasize that as an organization we place the utmost importance upon the integrity of our staff and insist on very high standards when it comes to personal conduct.

Miss Karlsson said that she understood this, and that as a British citizen she was reassured to hear of the high standards demanded of government employees. She added that in her most recent interview she had been told that she was being considered for a position in one of the intelligence agencies. Miss Karlsson said that it had long been an ambition of hers to work in this field as she had been brought up on stories of relatives across Europe being uprooted during the first half of the century and so enormously valued the stability and security provided by this country. She said that she would not do anything to jeopardize such an exciting possibility and would happily answer any further questions I might have.

Having set the scene, I explained to Miss Karlsson that we conduct extensive enquiries into the background of each applicant and that something of concern had arisen during this process. At this point I produced her file from my briefcase and reminded her that according to statements made during her previous vetting interview she was currently single but had had three intimate relationships in her life: at the ages of eighteen, twenty and twenty-seven. (I considered apologizing in advance for the sensitive nature of this topic, but determined that as Miss Karlsson is a confident and able young woman I might be better able to get to the truth of this issue by being direct and authoritative.) I asked her if she remembered this part of her first interview and she confirmed that she did. I then told her that our enquiries had raised the possibility that she was involved in a romantic relationship with a female acquaintance of hers, and offered her the opportunity to confirm or refute this allegation.

Miss Karlsson appeared taken aback by this line of questioning but quickly recovered her composure. She replied that it was possible I was referring to her close friendship with a young woman named Margaret DUKE. I asked her if their relationship was romantic in nature, and she replied by saying that it depended on what I meant by the word "romantic". I informed Miss Karlsson that I did not intend to engage in a semantic discussion and would appreciate it if she would give me a straightforward answer. She said that she had not intended to evade the question but that so much associated with the word "romantic" seemed more applicable to traditional male–female relationships. She said that she and DUKE did not go on dates and had never discussed a future together. However, she was extremely fond of DUKE and they spent a considerable amount of time together. During this time, they had kissed and engaged in other forms of physical intimacy. She asked me if this was an acceptable level of detail or whether I would like her to go further. (It occurs to me as I type this that there may have been some sarcasm in her words, but if so it was not evident in her manner at the time.)

I asked her why she had not disclosed this relationship in her first vetting interview. She said that the interviewer had asked about her relationships with men and so in her view she had answered every question truthfully. I said it was hard to believe that the interviewer had not asked a general question intended to elicit details of any other relationships, whether with men or women. Miss Karlsson replied that looking back, there might have been a question with this intention in mind, but that the wording was whether or not she had had "intercourse" with anyone else. She asked me if I had to hand the latest government definition of intercourse between women as this might help us clear up the matter. (Once again this strikes me as a sarcastic comment, but in a spirit of fairness to Miss Karlsson I did not think so at the time and merely record my observation here for the sake of completeness.)

I told her that I had no such definition to hand and that furthermore I understood very well that these subjects were difficult to discuss. However, it was important she made every effort to be transparent. I conceded that the inexperience of her first interviewer may have led to some genuine confusion on this topic and that I did not doubt her desire to be truthful, nor her integrity. Let us now be frank with one another, I said: did Miss Karlsson consider herself to be a homosexual? I explained that there was no moral judgement intended by the question but that Her Majesty's Government had concluded that homosexuals were more susceptible to blackmail by hostile foreign powers because they had to carry out their romantic activities under cover of darkness, so to speak. Whether we liked it or not, this was the reason they were not permitted access to the most sensitive reaches of government.

Having said that, I went on to explain that the government adopts an enlightened view on this matter and does not see it in black-and-white terms. In my professional experience, I explained, it is not uncommon to interview male candidates who had homosexual experiences at boarding school or even the occasional illicit encounter in adulthood. This is not a bar on their entry to government service, as long as they are honest and consider it a temporary deviation from an otherwise straight path. One swallow does not a summer make.

Miss Karlsson said that she was glad for this opportunity to set the record straight. She said that she had never before considered the question of whether she was homosexual as this had been her only relationship with another woman. She continues to feel attracted to men and expects that she will have more traditionally romantic relationships in future. She added that she hopes to get married and have a family one day. I thanked her for her honesty and said that in my view this episode should be recorded as an aberration on her part that could be swiftly rectified by taking the obvious steps. I reminded her that if successful in her application she would be subject to regular vetting reviews and so would need to maintain high standards of conduct throughout her government career, including in her personal relationships. I pointed out that future vetting officers would no doubt return to this subject with her.

We parted on cordial terms and Miss Karlsson thanked me for my visit. Her parents returned from their walk and we engaged in polite conversation on the doorstep before I made my excuses and left.

ENDS

One week after the above interview, we received a letter from Miss Karlsson in which she confirmed that she had terminated her relationship with Margaret DUKE.

We await your decision on whether to proceed with Miss Karlsson's application.

Yours sincerely,

J. Carson
Head of Vetting

SECRET

8B

Daily Press Summary
17 May 1985

Eastbourne Herald
Woman Killed in Cliff Plunge
By Derek Mann

A young woman was killed yesterday when she drove her car off the cliff at Beachy Head.

Horrified onlookers watched as the blue VW Golf accelerated out of the car park and raced towards the cliff edge. Wreckage of the car was located by police later that day and the body of a young woman recovered. She is believed to have died instantly.

The woman, identified locally as Margaret Duke, is reported to have moved recently to the area. She is not known to have any dependants. A neighbour told us that Duke had been heartbroken by the ending of a relationship and subsequently struggled with depression.

According to the Deputy Coroner, anyone driving over the cliffs "had very little chance of surviving". A post-mortem will be carried out later this week. A spokesman for the local council said that time will be set aside in the next meeting to discuss the installation of safety barriers.

NOT PROTECTIVELY MARKED

8C

20 November 1985

Dear Willa,

I received your note of 16 November with considerable alarm.

Are you really sure you wish to leave your current role and become a vetting officer? Are you aware that if you do this it will be impossible for you to return to the mainstream of the office? Vetting officers see highly personal information related to staff and so it has traditionally been the case that they are not allowed to work alongside colleagues whom they might have previously vetted. If you transfer, therefore, you will be turning your back on a wide range of possible roles. Do you really want to do this at a time when more and more areas are opening up to capable women officers such as yourself? Please reconsider! You are one of our stars, Willa, everyone can see that, and right at the beginning of what I have no doubt will be a long and glittering career. Playing a "vital role in ensuring the right sort of people join the office" is all well and good, but we need you out there on the front line!

PLEASE let's discuss further before you do anything rash.

Amelia
Deputy Director, Personnel

SECRET

CHAPTER NINE

Friday, 0018

"Leonard, what have you done? You've thrown Remnant into a complete tailspin. I know it's late, but you really need to come into the office and clear up this misunderstanding. I've tried to tell him there's a dozen innocent explanations for you visiting Willa in hospital, that he's already put you through an incredibly thorough loyalty test which you passed with flying colours. But over the course of a single day he's briefed the Director General that you might be a Russian agent, *then* that you're completely innocent, *then* that you've smashed up one of our flats, and *now* he's telling them all over again that you might be a Russian agent. He's saying you've made him look like a fool. Apparently he completely lost his temper with hospital staff for letting you see Willa. According to the nurse, she left the room for a while and when she came back in Willa was talking. Something about rotten apples, she said. He's jumped to the conclusion that this was a code and proves that you went there to receive instructions. I know this is madness, but you really need to come in and clear it up. We need you working on this too. You're the only person who's had face-to-face contact with the gardener, who, by the way, is at this very moment on a train approaching London. What's going on? Can you think of any reason he might be coming here?"

Friday, 0136

"Okay, you're asleep, I get it. God knows you need it after the week you've had. I assume you've checked into a hotel somewhere, because Remnant has sent people to look for you in every imaginable place – the operational flat, your flat, even your mother's house. They've been trying to reach your sisters too. Maybe you've got a girlfriend I don't know about. Anyway, if you *are* in a hotel, you need to be aware that the gardener – they've given him the nickname FROST HARDY – has arrived in London and checked in to a Travelodge by King's Cross, so if you're out in the open in that area at all tomorrow you'll need to be careful you don't bump into him. Or one of the several dozen surveillance officers they're sending out the door every minute. They found a rucksack in the woods behind FROST HARDY's cottage and it had a gun in it, albeit a pretty old and rusty-looking thing. But it looks like it's been fired recently, they're saying, which introduces a new level of risk, and so they've called in an armed surveillance team in case he's got another weapon with him in London. It's also the way he left so suddenly that concerns them. He was sitting on his sofa watching TV, went into the bathroom and came out holding a small transistor radio no one had ever seen before. Then he went into the woods behind the cottage. They had a camera inside a bird box that could just about see him putting in an earpiece, listening intently for about ten minutes and spending about another ten minutes twiddling a button. Then he jumped on his bicycle and made the last train for London with seconds to spare. Remnant thinks it's too much of a coincidence all this happened the same day Willa woke up from her coma. He's convinced you going to see her is also a piece of the puzzle. But of course it's also possible this is nothing to do with you or Willa and he's come to London to meet one of his other agents. Naturally they're flooding the hospital with surveillance, but the latest problem to be solved is that their radios interfere with medical equipment so they're going to have to do this the old-fashioned way, which everyone is complaining about. I have to say it's incredibly exciting, but I do wish you were here too."

Friday, 0355

"I'm glad someone's having a peaceful night's sleep. They ran out of things to do here about an hour ago. All the surveillance teams are in place and now it's just a question of waiting for people to start waking up. But Remnant can't sleep and so he had someone call in the operational psychologists to see if they could offer any insights, but they've spent the last few weeks chewing over Willa, FROST HARDY and probably you as well, and as a result they don't have anything to say that they haven't said a hundred times already. The only new thing in all this is that I've spent most of this week with you, and so they sat in a row and spent a full hour asking me questions

239

about it. Goodness, some of the questions. They asked if you ever seemed depressed, angry or unusually intense. I asked them if they'd ever met you. They made me go over everything step by step, and when I was describing the train journey and that little shit Daniels they wanted to know why he might have thought we were a couple. Maybe I'd been defending you a bit too much instead of jumping on the bandwagon. Anyway, we should get our story straight. I told them we had talked about having a drink at some point once this was all over but that it probably wouldn't happen. They asked if I was attracted to you. Can you believe it? I told them I thought you were an obnoxious prick. I'm just telling you this so you're ready for the questions when you come in. I don't know, I probably started blushing at some point. Especially when it came to that bit about me breaking you in half, and I started to think that… God, why am I even talking about this? It's too late for this sort of conversation. Shit. Shit. I don't even know what I'm trying to say. How do you delete this fucking thing?"

Friday, 0443

"This is the last one, I promise. Remnant has just sparked on the fact that you went straight from the train station to see Willa in hospital, and he demanded to know how you'd found out she'd woken up. After all that stuff with the psychologists he came straight to me. He was incandescent when I said I'd told you, and he read me the Riot Act about unauthorized disclosures and the penalties attached. I'm just letting you know in case you're not in the habit of routinely deleting your messages, or throwing your phone into the nearest available body of water…"

CHAPTER TEN

Friday, 0804

1

The ranking intelligence officer at the Russian embassy, more commonly known as the Resident, opens the front door of his London townhouse and steps into the warm sunshine of a new day. After yesterday's rainstorms he has dressed in his favourite grey suit, but as his skin prickles he realizes that even at this early hour it's too hot for wool and he hesitates, wondering whether he has time to change into something lighter. A tall and slender man, he pays careful attention to his wardrobe. With a sense of daring that marks him out from his more understated colleagues, he has purchased a linen suit the colour of the midday sky above the Italian Riviera, and he wonders whether today is —

One of his children is calling for him. That settles the matter. He pulls the door shut and hurries down to the —

A mobile phone lies on the wall at the front of his property. This isn't the first item he has found abandoned there. On one occasion it was a shoe, another time a glove, and there have been any number of cans and bottles. Once there was even a plastic bag filled with a startling amount of dog waste. He remains undecided as to whether that was an inconsiderate neighbour or a provocation by his British counterparts. But this phone is the most valuable item by far, and he pauses to look up and down the tree-lined avenue for its owner. There is nothing out of the ordinary there, certainly nothing to cause undue anxiety to a man of his vast experience – a man accustomed to the daily scrutiny of hostile intelligence agencies, a man trained to the highest level in detecting surveillance, a man who has been rewarded for his loyalty and service with one of the most prestigious posts in —

The phone rings. He bends from the waist and sees that the name of the person calling is … Ernesto. His half step backwards is quicker than he would have liked. He looks around again. Ernesto is not an uncommon name in an international city like London. It is the name of a delivery driver, or one of those workmen digging a hole at the end of the street. Like every other spy, the Resident engages daily in the study of coincidence, both those he places in front of others and those placed in front of him. He considers himself somewhat of an expert in this field, which encompasses (or so he tells his subordinates) the disciplines of psychology, statistics, aesthetics and philosophy. Recent questions he has addressed include: what does it mean to see the same face at two different points on one's walk to work? Is it plausible to be told that one's airline booking has been selected at random for an upgrade? Will a gardener find it suspicious if a hotel guest happens to leave a bottle of weed —

He has reached the end of the road. Today is the perfect day to test his invisible watchers with a new route and so he turns right instead of left. A queue stretches out of the local bakery and onto the pavement. The possibility of entrapment is always at the forefront of his mind. He never fails to be surprised by the number of Western diplomats in Moscow tempted into compromising positions. The bait is usually men or women, but there have been notable successes with drink, drugs and gambling. The British claim to be above such underhand tactics on their home turf, but he does not believe this to be true for a moment. It was only a few years ago that an SVR officer posted to London was sent home in disgrace by the ambassador when drugs were found in the tyre well of his car, and it is widely rumoured they were planted there by the British to discredit a talented officer in the middle of a delicate recruitment operation. Not just any drugs, either, but those popular with homosexuals. The rank and file were in uproar. To deliver a beating is one thing, but to smear the reputation of a good man like —

A car crawls past, a face turned towards him. Making a note of the number plate, he turns into a side street and picks —

It comes to him that this incident with the ringing phone could be put to good use. He has been looking for material to use in a lecture he hopes to be asked to deliver to graduates of the SVR Academy this autumn. It is customary for the Resident in either London or Washington to give the keynote speech. All his daydreams lead towards a podium and a large, appreciative audience. As important as the successful operation you have just concluded, he decides to tell them, is the energy and hunger with which you approach your next task. You must not dwell on your successes. Why, just a matter of a few weeks after closing the file on the traitor Kostya Bortnik, having succeeded where a dozen or more of my predecessors had failed, I was leaving my house one bright morning when to my surprise I found —

The one thing in his favour – the *only* thing in his favour, since the Resident in Washington, as everyone knows, has enjoyed a prodigiously successful few years – is that he has dealt with Kostya Bortnik just one year after the mass expulsion of intelligence officers (following that other unfortunate episode) hollowed out the London Residency. The expulsion has left him the equivalent, in terms of manpower, of the Resident of an obscure and unimportant embassy in a dusty corner of Africa. He has looked up the numbers. It wasn't always this way. When he was first told of his appointment, he quickly found out that he would have as many officers under his command in London as his equivalents in Stockholm, Oslo and Helsinki *combined*. He would have almost as many as Brussels, and they were responsible for NATO *and* the European Commission. But now? Now he has as many officers under his command as the Resident in *Angola*. He has two *fewer* than the Resident in *Chad*. His equivalent in Nigeria manages a team that is *twice as large*. He started to look up the numbers in South Africa but had to close the page as he felt his blood pressure rising. Three secretaries.

Three. The other day he had to do his own photocopying. The other day —

He steps into an alley that twists away from the main road and around the back of a supermarket. As it widens, he steps over shrubs into a car park and walks towards the front entrance, scanning the supermarket windows for anyone following him. He allows himself a rare moment of pride. Even with such meagre resources at his disposal, even putting Kostya Bortnik to one side, he has achieved things no one in Moscow expected of him, such as the recruitment of a prominent political journalist, a retired police chief superintendent, the private chef to a minor royal —

The doors slide open to admit him and he walks towards the rear exit, slowing to enjoy the air conditioning. Once outside he steps into a coffee shop and considers the sandwich selection while watching through the window to see whether anyone has hurried out of the supermarket after him. It is good to experience these small jolts of electricity, he thinks. At this point he would normally go directly to the embassy but decides that pausing for a few minutes will confuse anyone watching him and so he orders a double espresso, picks up a free newspaper and goes through to the toilets in the back for a few minutes of peace and quiet he rarely gets at home. The far cubicle is empty. He sits down and opens the newspaper to a story about London sewers. He is finishing the article when the door next to him clatters shut and he feels something tap against his foot. He lowers the newspaper and sees a mobile phone – the *same* mobile phone, he concludes afterwards – on the tiles beside his left foot. His startled reflection fills the black screen. It starts ringing. Once again the name Ernesto appears on the screen. He pulls up his trousers, kicks the phone away with some force and hurries out through the door and into the coffee shop while still fastening his belt. He is on the street by the time he realizes he's left his espresso behind. He turns into a busy pedestrian arcade. He is safe here. The embassy is less than fifteen minutes away. He knows who Ernesto is, of course – or Kostya, as he was called when they studied together at the Academy – but he also knows Kostya is the *last* person on earth who would try to contact him. It was a flawless operation, one he designed himself. The officer entered the country undetected, collected the poison from a cache in the garden of a stately home and left it in the hotel exactly as planned before flying out the next day. Since then the Resident has been checking the newspapers every day for news of Kostya's death. There is impatience in Moscow that it is taking this long. He hopes it will not affect his chances of being asked to deliver the keynote speech at the graduation ceremony. He has tried to tell them there is no way of knowing when Kostya will use the weedkiller. He has tried to argue that a little time between the agent's travel and Kostya's death is no bad thing, that it will confuse the British authorities. After half a dozen or more bungled, clumsy and violent attacks, he has told them, what was needed was a touch of subtlety. And it was under *his* leadership, after all, that Kostya was located after more than a decade out of sight. A trade attaché on holiday in

Norfolk saw him drive down a busy street at the wheel of a van emblazoned with the name of a country hotel. But still Moscow calls every day to ask whether Kostya is dead, and if there is not good news soon the Resident will be forced to come up with another plan. Moscow is obsessed with this. They have refused to green-light any other proposals until this matter is settled. Traitors must be dealt with, they shout down the line in a tone that insinuates failure is another form of betrayal, that if Kostya escapes this time the punishment set aside for him will be inflicted upon the person who let him get away, that that person's wife will find herself an outcast, this his children will grow up impoverished and —

He cuts across a patch of scrubby grass and turns at a trot into a housing estate. Why would *Kostya* call him? Has he found the poison? Has he taken the poison? Does he want the antidote? He hurries past a young mother pushing a pram. If Kostya is a dying man, does he plan to exact his revenge in his last hours by killing the —

The thought terrifies him and —

He breaks into a run through the estate towards the main road that will take him to the —

He wonders who the person in the neighbouring cubicle was. It can't have been Kostya, that would make no sense, so does that mean he has an accomplice helping —

Another young mother with a —

He swerves to avoid dog —

His breath comes —

A man but one so thin a stiff wind —

He looks back over his shoulder, sweating —

This wool, this wretched wool, although corduroy is no —

He crumples into a doorway. All the air has gone from his —

He feels as though he might throw —

The man leans over him, pats him gently on his cheek to revive him and presses a phone to his ear. He hears a familiar voice, a voice he never thought he would hear again in his lifetime, saying: "Dimitri, it's me. It's Ernesto, it's Kostya. We need to talk."

2

"You sound out of breath," says Kostya. "While you recover, let me tell you what we are going to do, for the benefit of both sides: we are going to sit down to find a way out of this mess. For my part, I have no problem admitting that I am in a very difficult position. The truth is that I never thought you would be able to locate me, Dimitri – I thought I had hidden myself forever from you and your friends. Your ruse with the weedkiller was clever, I grant you that. The bottle sat on my shelf for a few weeks and then one day I reached for it. I claim no credit for what happened next. It slipped from my hand and fell to the floor where the cat was sleeping. You can imagine what happened to the cat. I had to throw its body down a thirty-foot well, along with the weedkiller, and for seven nights after that I poured concrete down the well so the poison would be totally covered. At the same time, knowing you had discovered my location, I prepared to disappear once again. But on the seventh day an ambulance came to take away a cleaner who had complained of unusual symptoms. The next day it was the police. They spoke to everyone, including me. Particularly me – they have their suspicions, but what can they do? I have made sure over the years that nothing can be proven. So instead they have thrown a ring of surveillance around me —"

"Who is this?" says Dimitri. A good question, he thinks, a solid question. Stay calm. He will not be tricked into any admissions on an open line.

"You know very well who this is," says Kostya. "But in case you need proof, I will tell you that in our year at the Academy you were bottom in self-defence and I was top, a difference in ability that entertained the entire class one Christmas when after several hours of drinking the boxing instructor decided to put us in the ring together. I suspect that over the years you have found a way to use that elegantly broken nose to your advantage. I remember your shrewdness well, Dimitri. I remember how quick you were to call on your father's assistance after that regrettable episode on one of our training deployments overseas, and I very much hope you will be just as quick now to recognize an opportunity. Because I am waving a white flag, my friend. I understand that your efforts to kill me will continue until the day I die of old age, and therefore I wish to find a way to resolve this matter that satisfies us both."

"I don't know what you are talking about." Another solid response. He is doing well. He doesn't know what

Kostya hopes to achieve but it isn't going to work. He has come a long way since his days in the Academy, since that incident in Sweden that was so widely misunderstood.

"I am prepared to make a statement of apology and regret," says Kostya. "I am prepared to answer every possible question – even submit to a polygraph if the conditions are acceptable – to reassure you that I have not collaborated with the British during my years here. It is therefore incorrect to view me as a traitor. I have fled the battlefield, this is true, but not in the direction of the enemy camp. I understand the decision will not be yours. However, there is one decision that is yours, Dimitri, and yours alone, because this is the only time I will make this offer. Let me be very clear. If this phone call ends without an agreement for us to meet, you will never hear from me again. It will be another ten years before one of your men finds me, and when he does it will not be the body of a cat that I throw down a well in the middle of the night."

"I don't know who you are or what you are talking about," says Dimitri. He needs time to think. It is not hard to imagine how his seniors will respond when he tells them Kostya is alive. If he has to tell them he has rebuffed Kostya's offer to meet in person, there is no knowing what they might do. "Nonetheless, it is the duty of a diplomat to help his fellow citizens," he says mildly, "so I would suggest that you come to the embassy at your earliest convenience."

"So you can kill me? No, our meeting will take place in public. There is an additional element you must consider: as I have said, your ploy with the weedkiller has alerted the British authorities to my existence and as a result they are now following me. My skills might be rusty after three decades in retirement, but they have surrounded me in such numbers I would have to be blind not to see them."

"All this talk of poison and surveillance," the Resident says. He knows what Kostya is going to ask, but with almost no officers under his command it will be impossible to achieve. He has to find another way. "I don't know who you are, but I can assure you we wish you no harm. It certainly does sound like you need some assistance, though. If the British authorities are persecuting you, the Russian embassy is the right place for you. We can negotiate on your behalf with the British, should you so wish."

"I have just told you the British suspect me of being a Russian spy. What do you think they will do if they see me heading in the direction of the embassy? They will conclude I am trying to escape and arrest me on the spot. And if that happens, there is no knowing what I might say."

"What do you mean?"

"I have never broken the trust placed in me all those years ago. But if the British arrest me, if they threaten me with prison, I will have no choice but to tell them everything I know."

Dimitri struggles to imagine a worse outcome than this, that his subtle, intelligent, *artistic* plan involving a bottle of weedkiller ends up driving Kostya into the arms of the British. There is little doubt in his mind that for such a catastrophic failure the Kremlin would order his own death. But what can he do? Under these circumstances, how can he finish what he started? How can he assassinate someone being followed by British surveillance in London of all places? With no resources, with almost no officers? Even a month would be insufficient to make a plan. But a few hours? He needs time to think.

"Are you still there, Dimitri?" says Kostya. "The British will arrest me, I will tell them everything, and in return they will let me stay. But this is not my preference, Dimitri, and it should not be yours. You will have a difficult time explaining to your superiors that I offered you a meeting and you rejected it. We both know what they will do to you. I do not want to go down that route either. You may not believe this, but I took an oath of secrecy thirty-six years ago and have no wish to break it. That will only happen if you force me into an impossible position."

"My friend, my poor friend, whoever you are —"

"It gets worse, Dimitri. You were very easy to find. Look how easily I did it today, and with the help of a man who looks as though he plays the organ in a village church. Imagine what I can do if I turn to some of my more violent associates. Listen to me carefully, Dimitri. If you reject my offer of a peace deal, every future attempt on my life will be countered with an attempt on the life of whoever occupies *your* position at the embassy. If he is too well protected, I will simply go down the chain to his deputy and so on. This is not a campaign that will continue without your side incurring a cost. I will go to war against you. Is that understood?"

Dimitri knows how he must respond. "You are mentally ill and in need of urgent assistance," he says. "That much is clear. And it is my duty as your representative in

London to offer you a helping hand. Today is out of the question, however. I have pressing appointments. Let us say Monday morning at —"

"At three o'clock this afternoon I will be standing at the intersection of Oxford Street and Regent Street in the centre of London," says Kostya. "Have someone approach me to ask the time. I will follow this person at a distance and they will lead me to you. I would suggest a discreet cafe or a bench in a quiet corner of a park. I will not enter a vehicle, an apartment or a hotel room. If you are accompanied I will walk away. Most importantly of all, Dimitri, remember that I will be followed every step of the way by a British surveillance team. It is your job to get rid of them. Do you understand this? It is your job to get rid of them so we can talk freely. Now go and make your preparations. You have a busy day ahead of you."

FROM THE ARCHIVES

10A

Surveillance report/FROST HARDY
Friday 14 June 2019

0500: Change of shift.

0643: First sighting of FROST HARDY in lobby of King's
Cross Travelodge. He purchases coffee from a vending
machine and drinks it while studying a hotel tourist map
of London. He appears distracted. He is unshaven and
dressed in brown boots, dark green corduroy trousers
and a loose white cotton shirt. There is a square bulky
object in his front right trouser pocket that might be
the transistor radio he has previously been observed
using. He carries a khaki-coloured rucksack on one
shoulder.

0703: FROST HARDY leaves the hotel lobby and proceeds on
foot to St Pancras station. He goes directly to a Starbucks,
buys coffee, leaves Starbucks and waits for the nearby
disabled toilet to become free.

0722: FROST HARDY emerges from the disabled toilet and returns via the same route to his hotel.

Comment: There is no obvious reason for FROST HARDY's visit to St Pancras and Starbucks. The surveillance team's assessment is that he may have collected an item left there for him. A search of the toilet after he had gone indicated that a ceiling tile showed possible signs of having been moved.

0910: FROST HARDY reappears in the hotel lobby. He leaves immediately, walks to Euston Underground and takes the Northern Line southbound to Charing Cross.

0937: FROST HARDY boards the train from Charing Cross in the direction of Ramsgate in Kent. He selects a seat in a quiet carriage and reads a free newspaper.

1045: FROST HARDY disembarks at the village of Staplehurst. On the platform he produces an Ordnance Survey map from his rucksack and consults it for several minutes.

Comment: Previous searches of FROST HARDY's property did not turn up an Ordnance Survey map of this or any other area. It is therefore possible the map was among the items recovered from the disabled toilet this morning.

1051: FROST HARDY exits the station and proceeds south on Station Rd.

Comment: There is an immediate change in FROST HARDY's demeanour upon leaving the station. He appears to be more alert and frequently looks behind him.

1108: FROST HARDY walks out of the town, turns right onto Pinnock Lane and into the surrounding countryside.

Comment: FROST HARDY walks on a grass verge as there are no pavements and so officers are forced to keep their distance. The road narrows and twists and FROST HARDY frequently drops out of sight. Officers are deployed on bicycle to locate him. He is last sighted approx. 1.8 miles from the station. Shortly afterwards he takes advantage of a bend in the road to disappear from sight. Officers believe he climbed through a hedgerow. Reinforcements are called in and continue to search for over 30 minutes.

1142: FROST HARDY reappears on Pinnock Lane within twenty metres of the place where he was last seen. He walks at a brisk pace back to the train station.

Comment: FROST HARDY has grass in his hair and streaks of dirt on his shirt and trousers. There are what appear to be bee stings on his face and he repeatedly scratches one of his arms.

1204: FROST HARDY boards the next London-bound train.

ENDS

CHAPTER ELEVEN

Friday, 1500

There are ways to defeat surveillance, he will say to his audience. None of you here today should doubt that. A hostile surveillance team is constantly managing the tension between two contradictory requirements: to remain covert, and to remain in control of the target. The skilled practitioner, which is what all of you assembled here are on your way to becoming, can turn this against the enemy. Yes, there will be moments when they have you surrounded so completely that escape seems unimaginable. This is to be expected. They have the home advantage, after all. But there will be other moments, whether the team following you consists of ten or twenty or even a hundred people, when the only connecting link between you and that vast team, with all the resources of the state at its disposal, is one single surveillance officer with their eyes fixed upon the back of your head. This officer is followed by other officers who are followed by others still, like an arrowhead, or the wake behind a speeding – yes, this is better – it is like the wake left by a speedboat as it races across the ocean. And so if you happen to be walking along a busy thoroughfare, let us say, and with no warning whatsoever you turn off into an alley or a doorway, it is logical to assume that in these few seconds the thread connecting the surveillance team to you is at its thinnest, and it is at such a moment that I brought down the sharpest knife at my disposal to sever the thread that bound the traitor Kostya Bortnik to the British operatives behind him and release him into our loving embrace.

Pause for laughter, thinks Dimitri. Assuming he stays alive long enough to deliver this lecture, by this point his audience will be well aware of Kostya's fate.

He feels like throwing up. It is astonishing to him, in a thirty-year career during which he has traded so freely, so casually in the lives and deaths of others, that he has never stopped to consider what it must have been like for his victims. He feels like a new man, filled as he is with compassion for his dead, alongside a desperate wish that by the end of the week Kostya should be among them. Because if Kostya is not dead, Dimitri himself will be dead. It is as simple as that.

His phone vibrates with a message from Sergei, his right-hand man for this afternoon's operation. His usual job is in the embassy's mailroom. Sergei is on the ground with instructions simply to observe events and report back to Dimitri. The message reads: *Bird has taken flight.* Dimitri curses under his breath. It took an hour to assemble the team from embassy staff – some willing volunteers, others told they had no choice – which meant he was left with only forty-five minutes to explain the plan to them. The problem of working with amateurs is that you cannot take for granted they understand even the most basic principles of intelligence work. Take this text message, for example. Be discreet, he told Sergei. Although we will be using a secure messaging system, there is no need to mention anyone's name. And now this. Who would have thought he needed to explain that a code was pointless if both parties had not agreed in advance what it meant?

Anticipating such errors, however, he has designed the operation to account for the inexperience of the team. If anyone makes a mistake, someone else can step in. The only single point of failure will be the moment at which Kostya is grabbed off the street – that is the one part they can't attempt twice. Which explains why Dimitri is sitting in the back of a van in a side street not far from Speakers' Corner in Hyde Park. He will be the one to lay hands on Kostya and beat him into submission. It will cement his reputation as a man of action as well as of ideas. To help him he has taken a muscular man called Boris away from his job maintaining the fleet of embassy vehicles. A radio plays music in the background. The street has been chosen because it is quiet and there are no cameras, but also because it offers at its end a glimpse of the park to reassure Kostya that he is being led towards a secluded bench, exactly as he requested, rather than into a trap.

He looks again at Sergei's message. He takes it to mean that Kostya was standing where he said he would be at 3 p.m., that the new woman from Accounts approached him to ask the time and that at this moment he is following her at a discreet distance down Oxford Street. Things are going to plan. In the call this morning to Moscow, he barely got out the words that Kostya had called him and offered to meet before the most senior person in the room cut in to say that Dimitri should do *whatever* it took to secure Kostya's capture and fly him back to Russia for trial and execution. The relationship with the British is already so bad, his boss said, that there could not be a better time for an operation of such boldness. What can they do to punish us that they have not already done? The bullet is in the chamber. One way or another it will be fired.

Dimitri shifts position. His heart is racing, he feels like throwing up. He somehow found time to call his wife, but since he couldn't say anything over an open line, he found himself reminding her to collect his dry-cleaning, which caused her to snap at him and hang up. He is left burdened with all the things he wants to say to her and the children. "Papa", he heard one of them call out this morning, at which point he closed the door, at which point he hurried away.

He returns to his speech. It is the only thing able to distract him from the possibility of his own death. Where was he? I brought down the sharpest knife imaginable, he says to himself. No one would use those words to describe the team he has assembled. Besides, if the knife is sharp, where is the skill? No, what he has produced is a mallet. No, a hammer. Yes, much better. A Russian hammer. I lifted a clumsy, brutish Russian hammer and skilfully – no, that sounds unpatriotic – I lifted a mighty Russian hammer and —

His phone vibrates with a new message: *The bird has entered the nest.* This must mean the woman from Accounts has entered John Lewis from the east side, leading Kostya behind her, and that the three phases – the three hammer blows – of the operation are about to rain down on British heads.

It is necessary to keep your finger on the pulse of the society in which you are operating, he will say. You must understand where it is most sensitive, where it feels emboldened, where your knife will do most damage. No, where British bones will crack most easily beneath the force of your mighty Russian hammer.

He can't sit still for much longer. He shuffles to the back of the van and checks the peephole.

My weapon was not a Chechen criminal covered with tattoos. My weapon was a department store on a busy Friday afternoon. I took a venerable British institution and turned it against the British state. Pause for astonishment. Pause for appreciative nodding.

There are plans that evoke admiration whether they succeed or not. Even in failure they seem bold yet realistic, muscular yet pliant, laudable attempts to thumb the eye of the opposition. His plan does not fall into this category. If it fails, his plan – for it will be seen as *his* plan, even though Kostya determined the location and the timing, even though he has been forced to use imbecilic embassy staff – will be seen as laughable, as an embarrassment to his Service.

He checks on the driver. The side street they are on leads onto a busy road. From there they will proceed safely and slowly to the embassy compound. Their prisoner will be sedated by the embassy doctor and transferred to the back of a vehicle with diplomatic plates. At that moment, on the assumption that the British will have worked out what has happened, every single available Russian vehicle will leave the embassy at the same time and drive to different airfields. Only Dimitri and his prisoner will drive to Biggin Hill, where they will board a private jet on loan from an oligarch.

Just as tantalizing to Dimitri as the plaudits he will receive in Moscow for mounting such an audacious operation is the fact he will almost certainly be expelled from the UK. Yesterday he loved this country; today he hates it. The British will be embarrassed and lash out in the only way they know how. Dimitri will return to a medal ceremony and his pick of jobs anywhere in the world. Unfortunately he does not believe this will happen.

He consults his watch. The route on foot from John Lewis to the van should take no more than seventeen minutes. His phone vibrates: *Nest is on fire. Repeat. Nest is on fire.* What does that mean? Is it "on fire" in the way he intended? Or is it simply "on fire"? Why does he repeat the message if everything is proceeding according to plan? He curses Sergei and the hundreds of spy films he has seen. His phone vibrates again: *Bird is lost, bird is lost.* He throws up in the corner of the van. Boris shuffles back and looks through the spyhole. "Boss," he whispers, laying a large, sympathetic, oil-stained hand on Dimitri's shoulder. "Boss."

Dimitri elbows him aside and presses his eye to the peephole. The woman from Accounts is twenty metres from the van, and twenty metres behind her is the unmistakable figure of Kostya, wearing the hat and coat that were bundled into his hands as he slipped out of John Lewis. He can't see any sign of the British surveillance team behind Kostya. If they were still following him they would have concluded – because of what happened in John Lewis – that he was trying to escape, and they would have seized him, but the fact they have not done this surely indicates that he has escaped them.

Did I feel fear? Yes, I did. Did I feel nerves, uncertainty, doubt? My friends, my colleagues, my brothers: it may surprise you to hear that I felt all of these things. As the woman from Accounts draws level with the van, Boris grips the handle and prepares to slide open the door and leap out. Less than thirty seconds now. With trembling hands, Dimitri readies the medicated cloth to be pressed over Kostya's treacherous mouth. I am human, like all of you, he will say. I am made of flesh and blood. Is that the right note? Is it possible to be *too* humble? Dimitri is so busy wrestling with this important question that he doesn't notice a bicycle rickshaw coming the other way down the side street, pedalled by someone whose face he would probably recognize, whose corduroy suit he would definitely recognize, and he is still considering his speech when the rickshaw sails past the van and the woman from Accounts, and Kostya jumps into the back of it, and in a heartbeat he has turned the corner and disappeared from sight, and Dimitri is as good as dead.

FROM THE ARCHIVES

11A

Surveillance report/FROST HARDY

Friday 14 June 2019

1420: FROST HARDY takes the lift from his floor down to the hotel lobby. He is dressed in the same clothes as earlier in the day, still marked by mud and dirt, and carrying the khaki-coloured rucksack on his left shoulder. He has applied cream to the bee stings on his face. He proceeds to the reception desk and informs them that he wishes to check out.

1426: FROST HARDY leaves the hotel and walks directly to King's Cross Station, where he boards a southbound Underground train on the Victoria Line.

1452: FROST HARDY gets off the train at Oxford Circus. He takes the stairs to street-level and positions himself outside the Nike shop at the crossroads of Oxford Street and Regent Street. He looks at his watch frequently.

1501: A young woman approaches FROST HARDY and appears to ask him a question. FROST HARDY consults his watch and replies. Shortly afterwards, he begins to walk down Oxford Street in the direction of Bond Street. Surveillance crews note that the woman who appeared to ask FROST HARDY the time is walking approx. 10 paces ahead of him in the same direction. She is aged 30–35, dyed blonde hair, athletic build, wearing jeans, a brown leather jacket and carrying a green canvas tote bag. Covert photograph obtained.

Comment: Subsequent image analysis confirms that the woman works as a junior accounts manager in the Russian embassy.

1508: The young woman (hereafter Woman A) crosses Oxford Street and turns right down Holles Street to enter the John Lewis department store via a side entrance. FROST HARDY follows 10 paces behind her. The lead surveillance officer pauses briefly on the street outside to allow an elderly man to go through the doors first to create an air gap between himself and FROST HARDY.

1509: Woman A and FROST HARDY proceed into the store. Another woman (Woman B) approaches the elderly man who followed FROST HARDY through the doors and begins to shout loudly in heavily accented English that he has touched her. The elderly man appears confused and tries to distance himself from the screaming woman. However, he is prevented from doing this by a heavily built man accompanying Woman B who approaches the elderly man and knocks him to the floor.

Comment: CCTV footage subsequently obtained from John Lewis shows that Woman B and her male companion were clearly waiting by the door in order to intercept the first person who entered behind FROST HARDY. We have since identified the woman as the wife of the trade attaché at the Russian embassy and her male companion as the kitchen porter.

1511: Recognizing that this is a pre-planned tactic to deter surveillance and that FROST HARDY may be attempting to escape, the officer proceeds quickly through the doors, sidestepping the loud struggle between the elderly man and his assailant, and walks onto the shop floor in an effort to regain visual control of FROST HARDY as soon as possible.

1512: FROST HARDY is observed weaving through the displays in the men's clothing section.

Comment: Subsequent CCTV analysis shows two store security guards attempting to restrain the heavily built male, who has begun to punch and kick his elderly victim repeatedly. While this is happening, Woman B pays increasing attention to the surveillance officer who has just walked past her. Perhaps recognizing that she and her colleague have made a mistake, she runs after the officer and throws herself on his back, taking him by surprise and dragging him to the floor.

1513: Two additional surveillance officers enter John Lewis via the same entrance and observe the two attacks in progress. One officer goes to assist his colleague who is being attacked by Woman B and the other proceeds into the store to locate FROST HARDY.

1514: A young man standing on the escalator begins to shout that there is a man with a gun and that everybody should "run for your lives". Shoppers appear confused by this statement, particularly when the man changes his mind and shouts instead that the attacker has a bomb. Some customers begin to head for the exits.

Comment: Subsequent CCTV analysis shows that the young man on the escalator works as a property manager for the Russian embassy.

1515: Surveillance officers flood into John Lewis and attempt to cover the exits. FROST HARDY is briefly observed approaching the stairwell.

1516: The fire alarm sounds and customers and staff stream towards the exits. There is considerable confusion and panic as the young man on the escalator continues to shout that there is an armed "terrorist" in the building. FROST HARDY is sighted entering the stairwell.

Comment: Surveillance officers lose sight of FROST HARDY and are unable to regain visual control of him. All further events have been determined by store CCTV analysis.

1517: FROST HARDY is led down one flight of stairs by Woman A.

1518: A man at the bottom of the stairwell hands FROST HARDY a bundle containing a long coat and a hat.

Comment: The man is subsequently identified as the assistant cultural attaché at the Russian Embassy.

1519: Once on the basement level, FROST HARDY follows
Woman A to a door marked STAFF ONLY and from
there to the delivery bay. FROST HARDY puts on the
coat and hat and emerges onto Henrietta Place at the
rear of the building.

*Comment: Efforts are ongoing to identify the route taken by FROST
HARDY and Woman A after leaving John Lewis. The arrival of emergency services caused significant congestion in the area, limiting our
ability to fan out in vehicles to locate them, and crowds of passers-by
and shoppers outside the store meant that even on foot we were limited
in what we could do. Armed police arrived within 7 minutes and
began to secure the area and corral people streaming out of the store
(including many of our officers) as they suspected the gunman might
be among them. One surveillance officer tried to run from the scene
to rejoin the search for FROST HARDY but was tackled by a police
officer and temporarily arrested. Subsequent CCTV analysis shows that
FROST HARDY can be briefly sighted turning into Welbeck Way at
1526, suggesting that after exiting John Lewis he headed northwards,
and there is a possible sighting at 1538 on Fitzhardinge St, which
would put him and his accomplice heading west in the direction of
Marble Arch and Hyde Park. Our working assessment is that FROST
HARDY was picked up by a Russian official and so we are currently
reviewing ANPR and contacting car rental firms whose vehicles have
been sighted in the area. We are focusing in particular on roads in
the vicinity that are not covered by CCTV as these are more likely to
have been selected as pickup points. Priority leads to be followed up
include a tip-off from a member of the public who claims to have seen
someone hiding in a rubbish bin, a review of extensive social media
footage of the events inside and outside the store and a canvass of shop*

owners and local residents who might have seen a suspicious vehicle. We have also received reports of a stolen bicycle rickshaw observed moving unusually fast that was later found abandoned on a street corner several miles away.

CHAPTER TWELVE

Friday, 1700

The rusted orange Mini is tucked in behind an abandoned burger van in the part of the lay-by where the trees are thickest. Thirty feet away traffic races by. There's barely enough room for two people under the bonnet, so Leonard stands at one side. Ernesto scratches at the inflamed bee stings on his cheek.

"Are you allergic to bees?" asks Leonard.

He nods.

"It never occurred to me that a gardener might be allergic to bees."

Ernesto grunts. "I am sure you had a good reason for sending me there," he says, twisting a cable into a knot. He takes a penknife from his pocket and selects a tool.

"It's a good thing you know cars," says Leonard. "I had a hunch you would, the way you took that lawnmower to pieces on the lawn."

"That explains why you bought this."

"What do you mean?"

"The engine is about the same size. Tell me, how much did you pay for it?"

"Six hundred pounds."

Ernesto grunts again. "Try it now," he says.

Willa is sitting in the front passenger seat, wrapped in two blankets despite the warm evening air. Her slate-grey head rests weightlessly against the seat belt. Even since Leonard saw her in the hospital last night, new patches of skin have appeared through her thin white hair. He turns the key but the engine doesn't start. He rejoins Ernesto under the bonnet.

"Is she all right?"

"Just exhausted, I think," says Leonard.

"How did she get out of the hospital?"

"She climbed out of bed, put on a dressing gown and walked out of the front door. At least that's what I suspect happened. She wasn't under arrest, so there wasn't much they could do. If only all escapes were so simple."

"We haven't escaped yet."

"With a bit of luck they'll assume you're both on your way to a hero's welcome in Moscow and not even bother looking for you."

Ernesto straightens up and wipes his hands on his trousers. "That should do it," he says. He climbs into the driver's seat and speaks quietly to Willa.

"Leonard?" she says.

He walks around to her window. "Avoid motorways," he says, bending down, "and if you get the chance to switch cars again at some point on your way it'll help cover your tracks. I suppose in this thing" – he taps the roof of the car – "I needn't tell you to keep within the speed limit."

"Quiet, Leonard." Her breath comes fast and shallow but there is something she wants to say. "Having been responsible for bringing you into the profession, I now feel responsible for you leaving it."

He leans in further. Her breathing struggles like a car up a faraway hill.

"I'm sorry I won't be there to help you through it," Willa says.

Ernesto tries to hush her with a hand on her arm. A breeze teases a few white hairs from her head and carries them out of the window.

She gathers herself. "I've always thought it was one of the many clichés of our profession," she says. "That you can't leave. That you can't make a clean break of it." In the daylight her gouged, scarred skin has a lunar glow. "Look at the two of us," she says, reaching for Ernesto with her hand. "We might be the unlikeliest pair imaginable to tell you there is a life out there for an ex-spy."

"Willa," says Ernesto. "That's —"

"Quiet." It takes her a moment to refocus on Leonard. "I would like you to have more success than we have managed." She closes her eyes.

"He will be fine," says Ernesto. "He doesn't need advice, this one – in fact, he has already left, whether or not he has submitted his papers." He looks at Leonard. "You cannot be a spy and trust someone in the way you have trusted us. You must know it is at least possible that we have lied to you from the start."

"Ernesto," says Willa, "will you stop talking such —"

"You know this is true, Willa," says Ernesto. "You think *he* doesn't know this, that our entire story might be false? You cannot be a spy and take such a story as ours at face value. Their doctrine is that nothing on the surface has any value. The surface is a lie. The truth requires a shovel and the cover of darkness. The truth is always buried underground, like the roots of a tree, like a Roman coin, like —"

"Like a potato," says Willa.

"The truth exists in fragments, it exists underground."

"Come on, Ernesto, that's quite enough."

"No, this is the part he needs to hear. The surface can also be true if it is allowed the freedom to be itself. Hedges with corners, flowers in straight lines, not a weed in sight: the English garden is the ultimate lie. But if it is not tidied up too much, if the weeds are allowed their space, if the garden can express its own character, there is a truth there. Do you understand what I am saying?"

Leonard considers the question. "Maybe. I don't know, if I'm honest. Are we talking about gardens? You're the one who planted a Japanese maple in Norfolk, so I'm not sure how literally to take this idea of letting things run wild."

"Hear, hear, Leonard," says Willa. She looks at Ernesto. "If you don't stop talking I'm going back to the hospital."

"You've reminded me of something," says Leonard. He reaches into his bag for the cutting Ernesto gave him. "See if you can make it come to life on a wild and windy Scottish island."

Ernesto places it carefully in the passenger footwell between Willa's feet. He turns the ignition key.

"Leonard?" says Willa, raising her voice. "Is there anything you want to ask me?"

As it happens, there *is* something Leonard wants to know. There won't be a better moment to ask the question, and there won't be a better place – in this lay-by, behind that abandoned burger van, kneeling next to the open window of a rusted orange car. And Leonard is a man of questions. His ability to ask the right question at the right time in the right way is what has defined his career, and so this is the clearest sign yet that it has come to an end, for Leonard is lost for words.

Willa blows him a kiss.

The car lurches forward in a cloud of black smoke, takes the corner at surprising speed, and suddenly they are gone.

FROM THE ARCHIVES

12A

TOP SECRET

DATE: 9 July 2019
FROM: Gatekeeping
TO: Private Office

Director General,

These past four weeks have been without a doubt the hardest of my thirty-year career, filled as they have been with recrimination, accusation, embarrassment and profound regret. There have also been a few minor successes. If you will indulge me, I intend to begin with these.

My team has identified the Russian embassy staff members involved in the operation on Oxford Street. All ten have been expelled, with the exception of the kitchen porter, who was surprised to learn that he is not protected by diplomatic immunity and is therefore in custody awaiting trial for the manslaughter of an elderly male shopper. The effect on an embassy already hollowed out by the mass expulsion in 2018 has been catastrophic. Credible reports suggest a near total cessation of work of any kind across the Russian diplomatic mission, allowing us to downgrade the risk posed to the United Kingdom by Russia to the lowest level for decades.

Numerous social media postings concerning the events on Oxford Street have resulted in an outpouring of public condemnation, scorn and mockery directed towards the Russian state, consolidating the impression that their spies are malign and incompetent in equal measure. This will hinder their efforts to recruit individuals in this country and elsewhere who are willing to place their lives in such obviously unsafe hands. Speculation as to the reason for the incident has been rife. It is an understatement to say that it would be embarrassing if the truth became known, that this was an operation to exfiltrate their star illegal from under our noses, and so we have planted the idea with a few sympathetic journalists that its thwarted purpose was the kidnap of a Russian dissident, a story that comes close to the truth but happily misses the bullseye by a few crucial inches.

A side street near Hyde Park has been identified as the likely location in which FROST HARDY was picked up, by a bicycle rickshaw of the sort used to carry tourists around central London. We have recovered the disguise worn by the as yet unidentified Russian officer who piloted the rickshaw, in a rubbish bin directly outside the Russian embassy. An astounding blunder, confirming Russian responsibility for every element of this operation, but one in keeping with its amateurish tenor. We assess that FROST HARDY was likely transferred from the rickshaw to a vehicle and driven to Biggin Hill airfield, since records show that a private aeroplane belonging to an oligarch with close links to the Kremlin arrived unexpectedly at 1335 on the day in question and departed for Moscow at 1942 the same evening. A fleeting glimpse on Biggin Hill CCTV of the Russian Resident confirms that he also returned to Moscow, where he is no doubt being feted behind the scenes as the author of this coup de maître.

Willa Karlsson's escape from the hospital was a more straightforward matter. I bear responsibility for the fact there was no police officer posted outside her room. In the early days of this investigation, we were at pains to reassure partners such as the police that Karlsson's poisoning was not linked to the Russian state, to avoid the perception taking hold that we had yet another problem on our hands. All restrictions were directed towards visitors; we never imagined that Karlsson herself would try to leave, as we believed she had been the victim of a Russian assassination attempt and would want to stay in the hospital at all costs. Staff did what they could to persuade her to remain, but encountered "an extraordinary level of verbal and physical belligerence from a person in her condition" that meant there was little they could do. She caught a taxi on the street outside. We have tracked her journey to Islington – changing taxis three times on the way – but at that point the trail runs cold.

This has forced us to revise our view of Karlsson's role. As you know, we originally assessed that she was a Russian agent and that upon her retirement – at which point she ceased to be of use to them – they tried to murder her to cover up her betrayal. An exposure of her role would have led to a security review and the plugging of numerous vulnerabilities. However, Karlsson's disappearance on the same day FROST HARDY was flown back to Moscow strongly suggests that she accompanied him, which would indicate that she remained in favour with the Russian state she had served for so many years. For this reason, we are now exploring the theory that rather than being the intended victim of the poisoning, Karlsson may have accidentally ingested it while preparing to poison someone else entirely. We may have to wait until Karlsson is paraded across Red Square wearing a *ushanka* for confirmation of this theory.

All of which brings me to my concluding remarks. You will appreciate that it is extremely difficult for me to write this, but following our brief conversation this morning I have come to the decision that it is only proper to submit my resignation.

I began this letter by saying that the past month has been filled with recrimination, accusation, embarrassment and regret. This is true. But it is anger I feel most strongly as I write these words. Anger at Willa Karlsson, anger at Leonard Flood, anger at elements in this office who cannot see the ruination that lies around the corner, anger at you for allowing such an indisciplined culture to take root. I have been the victim of a cruel trick, and it pains me more than I can express to see my colleagues fall for it like a row of unthinking dominoes.

The intended narrative is plain to see. That on the day he intends to flee the country, FROST HARDY boards a train and travels to the same Kent village where I happen to live. That he dives through a hedgerow and disappears from sight only to reappear thirty minutes later with bee stings on his face and arms. That a folded piece of paper containing a grid of numbers and letters is later discovered inside one of my hives. I can read the writing on the wall as well as anyone else. It might as well have been daubed in giant red letters, in Leonard Flood's handwriting, on the side of my house: *Charles Remnant is a Russian spy.* The intent is equally clear: our enemies are seeking to dislodge me from my position. It pains me to say that by failing to offer me your wholehearted support you have inadvertently colluded in this most sinister endeavour. The only comfort I take is that my bees stung the Russian intruder repeatedly. "FROST HARDY has several visible bee stings on his left cheek." "FROST HARDY scratches at the bee stings on his cheek and arm." I have read and reread these words from the surveillance report hundreds of times. My bees, my army of bees – they fought to the end in my defence. If only you had shown one ounce of their courage.

I never imagined the time would come when I would be required to attest my innocence. For the record, however, I have never had any contact with a Russian. I have never done anything on their behalf or received any inducement whatsoever from them. Beyond the actions of FROST HARDY, there is not one single piece of evidence that points to my guilt. A police search of my house and property has not turned up anything of concern, and I note that an entire cohort of GCHQ mathematicians has been unable to crack the mysterious "code" – if I can dignify what is clearly a random jumble of nonsense with that term. The "optics", though, as you put it this morning, are damning. Staff are "confused", rumours are "rife". As you so generously explained to me, ours is a business that demands we sometimes act on judgements made with incomplete information, as though you found this state of affairs regrettable, as though you weren't thrilled to have finally found a pretext to get rid of me. "Live by the sword," you said, only stopping as you looked up and caught sight of the expression on my face. Die by the sword indeed.

It is not in my habit to dispute facts merely because they do not benefit me. More than anyone, I recognize that I have what you called a "credibility issue". The number of surveillance teams deployed on that day means that word of FROST HARDY's actions has spread to every corner of our community, making it impossible for me to retain the authority needed to do this most essential of jobs. I realized the truth of this myself when last week I attempted to interview an archivist suspected of stealing classified material, and the impertinent fool stopped just short of asking what gave *me* the right to accuse *him* of anything.

My blood was up then, I am not ashamed to admit it. I had to stop myself striking him. My blood is still up. I am not going to embarrass you or this office on my way out. But I am going to speak my mind. I have spent close to three decades bent low over the discipline files of this community, looking at the mishaps, the errors of judgement, the flat-out betrayals, and my conclusion is that we are at a fork in the road. In choosing the direction of travel, Director General, my counsel is that you must prize stability, steadfastness and continuity above all else. It is rarely voiced, let along set down in writing, but our hiring policy since the days of Vernon Kell and Mansfield Cumming has been to recruit individuals of a conservative bent. I am not talking about politics – in political terms, the opposite might be true – or even about society at large. I don't give a damn about society at large. They can do what they want. What concerns me here is this community of fewer than fifteen thousand. I have very strong feelings where they are concerned. I want to see them persist and endure, and the only way this will happen is if we continue to be extremely careful about who we allow in and equally rigorous about who we throw out. This means identifying anyone who has it in them to be a boat-rocker or a whistle-blower and ensuring our doors are shut when they come knocking. But we must go further than that. We must actively resist calls for change. We must stand back and let the winds of trend come and go. We must be a time capsule buried in the corner of the garden so that if things go wrong above ground we can continue working to protect the future of this great country. We must never be at the vanguard of anything. Let society rush around like an army without a general, getting into meaningless skirmishes it cannot win. What an army needs more than anything is a *rearguard*. By fulfilling this role we protect society's ability to retreat from misadventure, but only if we retain the essential character of a rearguard, which is to say that we must be cautious, sceptical, loyal, disciplined, ruthless and trusting only of our brothers in arms, no one else. Let others charge forward in expectation of an easy victory. We hang back muttering that we have seen this all before, that it won't end well, that before the day is out blood will be spilled.

In light of this, the only possible course of action is to fire with immediate effect the 247 serving officers in whose recruitment Willa Karlsson played a part. If Leonard Flood had not already resigned, I would suggest he was placed at the top of that list. We are still in the dark as to his role in all this, but his actions on that day – the destruction of official property, the unauthorized visit to Willa's hospital room, his disappearance from sight over the period during which the events on Oxford Street unfolded – strongly suggest he is not blameless. I know the arguments against firing 247 officers in one fell swoop. I have heard them countless times over the past few weeks, even from you. That it is too crude, that it is too cruel, that it will weaken morale, that among them are some of our finest and most effective officers. You are more concerned, you told me, with "building a tolerant workplace culture", with "recognizing and embracing diversity in its many forms", all of which, you fear, is inconsistent with a mass firing. Good for you. But the truth is that we will never know why Willa approved the vetting applications of those 247 officers. What we can be sure of is that she didn't hire them with *our* best interests at heart. Some of them will be good officers, placed there as cover, but others will be disciplinary time bombs waiting to explode. Others yet will be Russian spies. It will prove impossible to separate these categories one from the other until it is too late. A rot has set in: Jonas Worth, August Drummond and Leonard Flood, most recently, but there will be some who have inflicted unseen damage, and others who may yet bring this office to its knees.

I make no apology for the severity of my position. Let this be my final word as I close the discipline files for the last time. The orchard Willa planted must be cut down and burned. It will cause distress and suffering. But those who remain will be tall, proud and mighty oaks, the best this great country has to offer.

Charles Remnant OBE

TOP SECRET

TOP SECRET

Incoming call to Thames House
1622: 9 August 2019

BEGINS

LF: Franny? It's me. It's Leonard.

[Pause]

FS: Oh. The switchboard said it was … oh, I see.

LF: I would have gone for Mr A. Garfunkel but I thought they
    might smell a rat.

[Pause]

FS: Goodness, Leonard. You just … you just disappeared.

LF: I know. It's been a difficult couple of months. I thought
    it might be better for you if I kept my distance.

FS: Better for me? Why?

LF: The office has been exploring disciplinary charges against
    me. Or they were until I resigned, and then they brought
    the police in. It's all over now, they're not going to press
    charges. But I didn't think I'd be doing you any favours
    by picking up the phone.

FS: I heard rumours.

LF: I suppose that's inevitable in a community of professional gossips. What did you hear?

FS: Oh, just that you'd been arrested. I think someone might have seen you at a police station. Where are you calling from, Leonard?

LF: A phone box, if you can believe it. I intend this to be my last piece of professional tradecraft before I slip back unnoticed into civilian life.

FS: You and Remnant. Did you know he's gone too?

LF: I heard they'd given him an OBE. I assumed that meant he was staying.

FS: The DG threw an honour his way to ease him quietly out the door. That's what people are saying. There was no real evidence against him, nothing that would stand up in court. Just one little piece of paper covered with numbers and letters. Enough to blot his copybook.

LF: All these people leaving.

FS: All these people?

LF: Remnant, me, Willa and her Russian friend. I suppose I had in mind all those people Willa vetted as well. I know Remnant was trying to get rid of them.

FS: That hasn't happened. Did you know there are two branch directors among that group, not to mention a dozen or more section leaders? I think they're working through the list in a slightly more rational manner, refreshing background checks and reinterviewing. A few polygraphs too, I'm sure. It's all manageable. [Pause] How do you feel about leaving, Leonard?

LF: I wonder whether I had an expiry date stamped on me

somewhere and suddenly I just curdled. One day the thought of leaving was impossible, the next day it felt inevitable. Someone told me recently to be suspicious of the cliché that spies can't ever leave the job, so I'm trying to be positive.

FS: Did they manage to leave successfully?

LF: I don't think I'll ever know.

[Pause]

FS: You're a tough nut, Leonard. I'm sure you'll manage.

LF: If I get nostalgic I'll pop down to Kent to reminisce with Remnant.

FS: I'd love to be a fly on the wall at that reunion. Listen, it's really nice to hear from you. I'm glad you're okay. But I've got a busy day here.

LF: Have you been all right, Franny?

FS: Oh, well enough, I suppose. It's been good to have some time to let things settle. I think... I think maybe we both lost our heads that week.

LF: I'm not sure I've found mine yet.

FS: You will.

[Pause]

LF: One of the reasons I'm calling is to check that nothing I did caused any problems for you, Franny. You know, guilt by association. It's hard to avoid in our business. Or in *your* business, I should say. Sometimes so little is known about a situation that the smallest of hints one way or another can take on huge significance.

FS: As Remnant found out to his cost.

LF: I hope he's okay too, I really do. But I feel a greater sense of responsibility to you.

FS: That's kind of you. I'm not aware of any problems. Behind the scenes, though? I've never asked the question because I know I wouldn't get a straight answer. That's one of the problems with spies running an HR department, they end up behaving as though it's wartime and they're operating behind enemy lines. Sometimes it feels as though you'd have to break into their files in the middle of the night just to get a straight answer about holiday pay or overtime rates.

LF: I've made it clear repeatedly that you weren't involved.

FS: Involved in what exactly?

LF: This probably isn't the place to go into details.

FS: I'll make do with the rumours then.

LF: What are they?

FS: Top three, in reverse order? Nervous breakdown, drink problem, Remnant was right all along and you were a Russian agent.

LF: What do you think?

FS: I'm pushing a fourth option. Hard to get much traction though.

LF: What is it?

FS: You and your questions, Leonard. You haven't got a professional licence to ask them any more, do you know that? It's been revoked. Let me ask you something instead. Whatever it was you did, do you think it was the right thing?

LF: I don't know. That week's all a bit of a blur. It's like the deck has been shuffled and those cards have ended up on the far side.

FS: Which cards are on the near side?

LF: That's a hard question to answer, Franny.

[Pause]

FS: Maybe too personal as well. I'm sorry, Leonard. It doesn't matter. I really should go.

LF: I've been thinking about this time when I was a boy and I threw a rock through the window of the local church. The priest caught me running away and called the police. My mother didn't have the money to pay for a new window, so I worked for a year looking after the graveyard – weeding, cutting the grass, clearing away dead flowers. Willa asked me about it in my vetting interview. I think we got there through a question about being in trouble with the authorities. She wanted to know everything. What the names on the gravestones were, how old the people were when they died, if I ever talked to them, what I said. She told me about a friend of hers who died, Margaret, I think that was her name. It was a car accident. Anyway, her parents had her cremated and they wouldn't tell Willa where they'd scattered her ashes, so every year on the anniversary of the accident she'd go and sit on the cliff where it happened and dangle her legs over the edge. She said that at first she'd been angry with them for not burying Margaret properly in a churchyard but that she'd come to love that feeling of sitting on the cliff. Like she could blow away at any moment, she said. Or turn into a bird. We must have talked about it all for a good half hour. Margaret was the reason she became a vetting officer, she said. It wasn't what I'd expected, none of it was. To be honest, I'd half made up my mind not to join, but Willa was so … so unusual, and so kind to me, that I went ahead with it.

[Pause]

FS: What do you think it was all about, Leonard?

LF: The case? I don't know. I've got such a slippery grasp of the facts that I might be the worst person to ask. I think the gardener was mostly a gardener, at least these days. I think if Willa was a Russian spy it lasted for about five minutes. I think something happened early in her career to make her angry, but also a bit less cautious maybe, a bit less suspicious and scared of the outside world than some of her colleagues. She certainly loved oddballs and outsiders. She took delight in people who had it in them to be naughty. She thought they made an organization stronger. There's a passage underlined in one of her books, something about people who make "new and manifold experiments", about the way they might inflict a wound on a community but ultimately make it healthier. I think that's the closest I can get to it. She wanted the Service to be braver than it is. She wanted it to be better. [Pause] What's the fourth option, Franny?

FS: What?

LF: The fourth option you're pushing. About what I did.

FS: It'll only make sense if I'm right.

LF: Let's hear it.

FS: That you had a *Blade Runner* moment. That you wanted to find out if you were a human or a replicant.

[Laughter]

FS: It's nice to hear you laugh, Leonard. I'm not sure I've heard much of that before.

LF: I'm going away, Franny.

[Pause]

FS: Where?

LF: The East Coast of America. There was a reforestation

project I was going to work for before I joined the office. Before Willa changed my mind. I'm not sure there's even a project any more. Even if there's not, I thought I'd go and have a look.

FS: A look at America?

LF: See what all the fuss is about.

FS: Makes sense. After all, you did write a song about that, Mr P. Simon.

LF: Is that the one about a Greyhound bus?

FS: That and a spy wearing a gabardine suit. Maybe that's where you went wrong. Too much corduroy. [Pause] I guess this is goodbye, Leonard.

LF: I do have one last question for you. If you can stand it.

FS: There's always one last question with you, Leonard. Let me guess. Is it about Remnant's replacement? You won't believe who they've appointed. Or —

LF: Franny, I —

FS: Or who's got *your* job, or what they've done with that flat you smashed up, or the truth behind that story in the papers about the bug in —

LF: Franny, will —

FS: The *alleged* bug, I should say —

LF: Franny. Franny. Wait.

FS: What?

[Pause]

LF: Will you come with me?

EPILOGUE

It was a full six months before three intrepid canoeists nearing the end of a tour down Scotland's east coast were blown onto a remote wooded island no larger than a football pitch, and another three days before the storm abated sufficiently for them to get to a pub on the mainland and describe what they had found there, and a week or more for someone to mention in passing to the police that squatters might have taken over some public land, and then another two weeks before an officer set foot on the island, on a day so warm and bright that she couldn't look at the waves without squinting.

What she found was a crofter's cottage built at least a hundred years earlier, very much like dozens of other cottages all along that coast. The first thing she noticed was the wind turbine, secured precariously to the top of the roof, built from the oddest assortment of timber, scrap metal and plastic bottles, and held together with twine from a salvaged fishing net. Newly crafted wooden shutters covered the windows and a vegetable garden had been planted in the eastern lee of the cottage. On the kitchen table a handwritten note invited any visitors to the island to take full advantage of the well-stocked larder, the firewood, the outhouse and the small library, adding that for anyone staying overnight the most comfortable bed by far was in the room at the end of the corridor upstairs, and suggesting it would be worth leaving the shutters open so as to be woken by the sunrise.

There was more. A hutch had been constructed not far from the cottage, and the police officer reported that up to a dozen surprisingly friendly rabbits came out of the woods to see who had arrived. A rowing boat tied to a tree showed signs of extensive repairs. A shield of branches stuck into the earth protected a young sapling of distinctive colour from the worst of the wind. When the officer had first stepped off the boat and followed the path up through the trees, she'd twice tripped on roots that stuck out above the ground, and it was only once inside the cottage that she realized the roots were somehow connected by a rope that ran through a series of underground pipes to a bell that rang loudly by the front door to warn those inside that visitors were on their way. A roughly hewed stone had been placed on the highest bluff of the island. The officer considered what she knew about by-laws and the use of public land for burials, and made brief and unsuccessful attempts to locate a body before concluding that there was nothing to confirm it was a gravestone, and therefore didn't merit further investigation.

That might have been the end of it. A file in a cabinet somewhere contains her report. A few days later a senior officer added something by hand that I'm ashamed to admit I can't quite make out, despite my thirty-two years in the archives. There used to be so much handwritten material passing across my desk that I could decode any scribble at first glance. These days everything is typed and printed, which certainly makes things easier for someone in my position, but I would happily return to the old days just to get away from the impression left by these many thousands of perfectly legible files that *everything makes sense.* Nothing could be further from the truth. This vast archive is a repository of loose ends. I've never come across a file that contains a satisfying conclusion, one that answers all the questions that went before. Jonas, August and now Leonard – the stories I have told are part theirs, yes, but the rest is all mine. I certainly make no claim to accuracy. I never met them, and if we passed each other in a corridor I didn't remark on the fact. Down here alone at night, once I have no writing left in me and my life's work is back in its hiding place on a high and dusty shelf, I make sure to take down a file at random, and it never fails to thrill me, that first encounter with the stray fragments and misunderstood snippets of a person's life, the yellowing pages noisy with accents, registers, ranks and voices that at rare moments might come together to form a choir but more often than not are a street fight squeezed between the covers of a government-issue file. Every one of these stories can be read a hundred and one different ways.

A week or so after the police officer's visit another note was added to the file. It suggested a possible connection between the island's mysterious inhabitant and a sighting by a coastguard helicopter of a small sailing boat almost a hundred miles away. Cloud cover that day was low and thick, so the pilot couldn't be sure, but she reported seeing at least one dog on board, and either one or two people, and so many plant pots that the boat looked like a floating garden. She circled lower in an attempt to see its name, worried about the storm front moving in quickly from the east, but strong winds and a flock of pink-footed geese forced her back. When she returned to the area the next day the boat was nowhere to be seen. So they updated the file, and kept it open for a year or more after that in case anything else turned up, but nothing did, and no one likes an open file, I know that better than most, so it was closed along with the investigation, and life moved on.

ACKNOWLEDGEMENTS

I have been remiss in waiting until my third novel to acknowledge those who have helped along the way.

Huge thanks are due to Georgina Capel, Simon Shaps and their team, super-agents of the non-lethal variety. François von Hurter, Laurence Colchester and Alex Hippisley-Cox at Bitter Lemon Press have displayed bottomless energy and enthusiasm, and Sarah Terry's forensic eye has picked up many an unforced error. This book looks as good as it does on the outside because of Aaron Munday, and as sharp as it does on the inside because of Alex Billington. I am grateful to Annabel Merullo for opening the first door. My early readers, most assiduously Tom S., have made this book better than it was, and my first readers, also known as The Government Censors, have made it shorter. They would like me to remind you that everything you have read is made-up, fictional, fantastical, entirely the product of its author's fevered imagination, with little or no grounding in any recognizable reality.

And to my family, near and far. Thank you – I feel very lucky.

ABOUT THE AUTHOR

James Wolff grew up in the Middle East and now lives in London. He worked for the British government for over ten years. *The Man in the Corduroy Suit* is his third novel.